Molly Wyer studied creativ
College, University of London. Jne has written, edited and
made tea for a variety of nonprofit organizations. She lives
in Arroyo Grande, California, and is the sole sister in a large
family of brothers. This is her first novel.

After the Storm

by

Molly Wyer

To Keith, Erin, Deming + Kendall, who all know Baja better than I do!

Love,
Molly Wyer

©2020 Molly Wyer
ISBN 0-936315-46-6
STARHAVEN, 42 Frognal, London NW3 6AG
books@starhaven.org.uk
www.starhaven.org.uk
https://www.facebook.com/starhaven.org.uk/

Typeset in Palatino Linotype

"Sleep after toil, port after stormy seas,
Ease after war, death after life, doth greatly please."

The Faerie Queene, Book I, Canto 9
(The knight of the Red Cross is tempted by despair)

I.

We were at my dad's wake talking to Uncle Ernie, when he sprung it on us: "You know, it kills me that your dad died before the trip panned out." He raised his glass and took a long drink of Stella. "No pun intended, Dave."

"What trip?" I said.

"His birthday trip to Panama." He looked at Dylan and me, blue eyes needle-sharp. "He didn't tell you? He wanted the three of you to go on a sailing trip for his 60th birthday. And – you know."

I could see my blank stare reflected on Dylan's face.

"He wanted you two to get over your Jacob and Esau complex."

Dylan snorted. I glared at him, but then his grin melted in weird directions. I looked away.

Uncle Ernie pressed on: "He even bought the boat."

I sucked in beer bubbles, which gave my eyes an excuse for watering. By the time I was done gasping for breath the conversation had moved on, but the boat was out there, drifting through all our thoughts.

The seminal phone conversation went something like this:
"Hey Jim."

"Hey Dylan... What's up?"

"Want to go sailing? I was thinking you could meet me in San Diego, since Panama is pretty far south."

I pulled the cell phone away from my ear and stared at the number. It really was Dylan. "What?"

"Panama. It's far away."

"I know. Are you high?"

"No."

"Panama? Like, Dad's sailing trip?"

"Why not?"

"You're crazy."

"Is that a no?"

I drew a long breath in through my nose. "I'll think about it."

"Really?"

"Yeah. Why not? But that's all I'm saying I'll do."

"Okay."

I was intrigued in spite of myself: "You think we can sail the boat he bought? It's been years since I've sailed at all."

"Well, you read up on navigation and I'll make sure we have what we need on board. But we're doing this old school. No GPS and shit."

"To be clear, so far only one of us is 'doing this'. I'll read some resources on celestial navigation, but I'm not sure about going without a backup system – *if* we go."

Dylan had kept right on talking: "Uncle Ernie said the boat's docked in Mission Bay, so that makes life easier. And my boss says I can take up to six months off, no problem."

"You're crazy."

"I'll take that as a yes. Put in for some time off work."

"I still haven't said I'll come."

I didn't bother telling him I'd quit my job when I found out about Leslie and Stefan.

I watched streaks of blue on blue flashing past the train window. Today the ocean's blue was the kind you could stare at for hours – thirst-quenching blue. The sky was pale by contrast, but so clear you almost expected to see through to the stars. The train snaked closer to the coast and I spotted two dolphins weaving through the swells. It was 10 a.m. on a weekday and not too many surfers were out at Rincon, but one man on a paddleboard caught a wave and sliced toward the shore at a diagonal, using his paddle like a rudder. That glide made it seem effortless. Oil rigs, Channel Islands, dolphins, surfers, all blurred together. The gentle hush and roll of the train soothed me faster than a sleeping pill.

When I stumbled out in San Diego, I felt like I'd been drugged. Hours of sleep had only whetted my appetite for more, reminding me how bone-achingly tired I was.

Dylan was pulled up to the curb, waiting for me in his Ray-Bans and his cherry red convertible. I slung my bag into the back to the accompaniment of Girl Talk. The bass was up so loud that the car shuddered back and forth. I barely had time to make contact with the passenger seat before we squealed away from the station.

"Hey."

"Hey." Dylan kept his eyes on the traffic. "Glad you made it."

There were a few minutes of silence as we threaded surface streets and merged onto the I-5. Then Dylan started talking again, over the wind rushing into our faces: "I saw the boat. It's a sweet 44-footer. And Uncle Ernie's letting us borrow some of his spare spearfishing gear. So we can live off the land – ocean." He smiled without much commitment.

"Cool. We pick her up in Mission Bay and head south?"

I tried to keep the skepticism to a minimum. But I hadn't been on a real sailing trip since that summer in college when we sailed down to Catalina Island – and I didn't think Dylan had, either.

"Glad to see you're so convinced this is going to work." He shifted gears and sped up.

A few days later, we set off with the morning tide. The coastline began to recede. I looked at Dylan. I should probably have been worried, but I had the bittersweet tang of the sea in my nose and its siren call was upon me. I couldn't hide a smile.

"How about some music?" Dylan pulled out a dusty, battery-powered stereo and stuck a cassette in. James Taylor started singing about Mexico, and I dug a couple bottles of Pacifico out of the ice chest.

"Oh, Mexico, it sounds so sweet with the sun sinking low..."

"Remember when Dad used to sing that song?"

My eyes jerked away from the front of the boat to my brother. Dylan was scanning the horizon carefully, though I was the one steering.

I nodded, then took a long drink, feeling the golden liquid tickle the corners of my mouth before I swallowed. "Remember driving to Uncle Ernie's in that ratty old Volvo – through Mexicali, San Felipe, Puertecitos – and that one tape playing over and over?"

"I've never really been so I don't really know..."

"What else was on there?"

Dylan scratched the back of his head, which made his thick brown hair stand out like it had when he was a kid. "'Margaritaville'... 'Take It to the Limit'... 'Operator'... 'Surfin' USA'."

Hearing the names of those songs, I could smell diesel and burning trash and feel the corduroy road bumping along beneath the three of us.

Then the song changed. Leslie and I had slow-danced to this one. I could still feel her lips brushing my ear as she sang, *"Run like poison in my blood."* I leaned over to the cassette player. "Kinda hate that song. Mind if I skip it?"

Dylan shrugged.

I pressed fast forward and watched the little wheels spin in the tape deck, till I remembered I was supposed to be steering our vessel.

Once we made it through customs in Ensenada, I realized this might really be happening. We didn't know when we'd next anchor near civilization, so we stocked up on staples: ice, beer, limes, tortillas, cilantro, and avocados. Dylan also insisted that we stop at a *panadería* on our way back to the boat, even though our hands were full with the groceries we already had.

We walked out with arms stuffed with fresh *bolios*.

"See?" said Dylan. "Worth it."

Between mouthfuls of warm bread I agreed that he might be right – this time.

"I'll take what I can get." Dylan elbowed me, a little harder than necessary, after a minute: "Food coma already?"

I drew a long breath. "No, I'm good… Actually, I was just remembering how much Baja used to scare me as a kid."

"As a kid, huh?"

"What's that supposed to mean?"

"Nothing. I just noticed you getting a little tense when we saw those *Federales* packing – whatever guns they were packing."

"Well I don't come from the hood like you do. I'm from San Luis Obispo, where you're more likely to see a man burn himself alive than get shot."

Dylan frowned: "Yeah, I heard about that."

I didn't know why I'd brought it up.

He latched onto another phrase: "What do you mean I live in 'the hood', anyway? Last time I checked, Carlsbad isn't the hood."

I kicked at the dirt: "Pretty much anything is going to be more 'hood' than SLO. But that's not important right now. The real question is, what are we going to call this boat of ours? I don't like the name *Nelly*. Can we at least rename her *unofficially*?"

Dylan took the bait.

I woke up the next morning feeling sticky; I dragged myself out of my bunk and up the few steps to the fresh air. We really needed to start sleeping on deck – it was too hot in the cabin. The sky was dusty pink over warm brown mountains. I'd wrestled out of my shirt in the night, so I jumped right over the side, boxers and all. The water only felt cold for a few seconds. I ducked my head under and swam a few laps around the boat. Then, treading water and slapping the hull, I hollered for Dylan. A couple of muttered curses preceded his tousled head out of the cabin.

"Damn it, Jim! Haven't you heard of sleep?"

I spat an arc of water in Dylan's direction and backstroked a few feet. "Fine, go back to bed if you want." I wasn't really sure why I'd felt the urge to wake him.

"Well, I'm up now." Dylan scowled. Then, with a running leap, he cannonballed into the water just beside me.

"Thought I was far enough away." I blew water out of my nose.

"That's your problem, you always underestimate me."

I looked at him for a moment. The taller, broader-shouldered brother with the strong cheekbones and good tan. Yes, I *must* underestimate him.

We trod water in silence, watching the sun burst over the mountains like it was the first time.

Dylan spoke after a couple of minutes: "So, what's for breakfast?"

"Oh, so I'm making breakfast?"

"Hey, you woke me up – you *must* have a good reason."

After some exceptional eggs and bacon – it was time to use up all the bacon – I suggested taking the zodiac around the bay to see if the fish were biting.

The steely sheen on the still morning sea and choke of the motor reminded me of the first time I caught a fish all by myself. Of course there were plenty of trips to Hume Lake or the Lopez trout farm when Dylan and I were little, but we'd always had help reeling the fish in, or at least hooking them, once we got a little older. But when I was nine or ten and Dylan was eight or nine, Dad decided we were ready for the *real thing*.

We crammed Dad's old silver Volvo full of supplies and headed down to visit Uncle Ernie, who has a place in Baja, not far south of Puertecitos. Don't get the wrong idea, though: it's no glamorous vacation home, nor does he want it to be. Uncle Ernie's place is a trailer that he's built onto over the years with scrap lumber and plywood and spare toilet bowls – anything he comes across that he can repurpose. It took eight and nine-year-old Dylan and I a little while to get over the fact that we had to flush the toilet with a bucket of saltwater – and that our beds were cots on the sand ("Don't let the coyotes get you!" Uncle Ernie said). Pretty soon we couldn't get enough of it. Digging for clams, watching for shooting stars at night, sitting around the fire pit listening to Dad and Uncle Ernie swapping stories about Baja in their young lawless days, kayaking, swimming ...And, best of all, fishing.

We'd get up when the sun was blazing on our sleeping bags from across the bay (and the flies were buzzing too persistently for us to sleep anymore), eat cold cereal on the patio while Dad and Uncle Ernie woke up over coffee and then – if the wind was down – we'd 'help' get the dinghy down to the water.

The sun had you sweating as you waited in the boat, then the engine caught and the dinghy purred out into the bay. Maybe you went hunting for rays or maybe you sped straight off for the bass hole. Either way, you weren't hot anymore, because the wind from the boat's forward motion slapped you in the face and you had to hold on to your Padres baseball cap. The water was smooth and shiny as silk, and you seemed to be flying away from the multi-colored houses that lived along the horseshoe of the bay, towards the great unknown of the eastern horizon.

The boat stopped when Uncle Ernie smelled fish, and you dropped your line in and tried not to catch the bottom, and the sun was hot again on your shoulders and time seemed to hold its breath – until the line wriggled. The first few times I felt that tug, I panicked and didn't reel in nice and easy, which meant I lost at least three fish. I could hear the irritation in Dad's voice, asking if I wanted help reeling in the next one.

"Give him another chance – he's getting it," said Uncle Ernie, who'd been hollering just as loud when I had the last one on the line. "Why don't you take my pole, Dave, and I'll get Dylan's line off the bottom?"

Then it happened. While my line was dropping back down to the bottom, it gave a shiver and started pulling away from the boat. I started reeling – firm but not too fast – fighting to keep the pole up off the side of the boat. The butt dug into my stomach and my arms shook, but I kept reeling, spurred on by yells from Dad, Ernie, and Dylan.

At last Dad said: "Stop! Now bring him this way!"

He scooped the struggling fish up with the net, untangled the hook from its jaw and held it up, dripping, for everyone to see. It was whitish with dapples of brown and big eyes and heaving gills.

"I thought he'd be bigger," I said.

"No, he's solid. Two pounder, I bet. We can have fish tacos tonight, if we catch a few more!" Uncle Ernie gave me a nod of approval.

I felt sorry for my fish as he was thrown into the bucket instead of back into the ocean, but I also felt a glow of pride. We would eat *my* fish tonight! And I had caught it all on my own. With an inward thrill, I let the line spin out past my thumb and into the water again.

"Think we'll catch some corvina?"

"Sure, yeah!" I shrugged off the memory, still so tangible I could feel the weight of the pole in my hand, though Dylan and I hadn't picked a spot to drop our lines yet.

"*Someone* hasn't been reading up on their banned fish."

I looked up in surprise.

"Wait. You can't keep corvina anymore?"

"Nope. They're protected now – too many people raping the ecosystem down here for too long, I guess."

"I can't believe it!" I said. "Those were the first – "

"...First big fish we caught. Yeah, I remember that day." Dylan cut the motor and handed me a rod. "I think there's something here." The water dimpled seductively.

We cast and reeled, cast and reeled for a while in silence.

"Think we've drifted off the spot," I said.

Dylan cast again: "Have a little faith."

I rolled my eyes and cast. A minute later, I felt that first experimental tug on the line. I forgot about Leslie, forgot what had dragged us down here – even forgot to be peeved that Dylan had been right after all. For a moment, I was the old man in Hemingway's tale, alone with the sea.

"Not too fast, Jimmy! You're gonna – "

"*Damn.*"

"Don't worry, there'll be – oh!" Dylan's line jerked. "I think I've got a bite."

The line twitched and then ceased moving.

"Shit!" He spat the word into the glassy water.

I turned away to hide a graceless smile, but Dylan caught me out of the corner of his eye. He reeled his line in carefully, turned the dinghy around, and motored back to the sailboat.

I flopped onto the sand, panting. It must have been a couple of years since I'd last swum properly, and my muscles felt rubbery from the exertion, although the boat wasn't anchored *that* far away. I let the sun compete with the lapping waves to see whether I would dry out or not. Why was I being such an idiot? Here I was, flirting with the monsters of the past, when Dylan seemed willing to play nice. I closed my eyes. I needed a few minutes of not thinking at all, of just the sun on my shoulders and the eternal whisper of the ocean against the beach.

I rolled onto my back and blinked up at the sky. I must have slept. The sand beneath me was still damp, although the tide had retreated and left the rest of me to dry in the sun. I lifted my head just far enough to look out at *Nelly*. (We still had agreed on no better name for our boat.) No movement on board. Dylan was probably sprawled out in the sun with a PBR – the Pacifico was just about gone – not giving our earlier skirmish a thought. I should do the same. Filial harmony: that's what Dad had wanted for us, right?

Dylan had always been better at separating his emotional responses from the rest of his life. He refused, for example, to let his fear of stingrays keep him from learning to snorkel. Of course I learned to snorkel too, but I wasn't deathly afraid of stingrays like he was. I didn't learn to waterski though, because I couldn't get over my fear of being dragged along under water – as had happened the first (and only) time I'd tried it. And I think that was a mark against my manliness, in Dad's eyes.

Anyway, it was easier for Dylan to be cool about our past because he'd always come out ahead. Just one example: upon my graduation from Cal Poly, I landed a job with a green energy startup in San Luis Obispo; when Dylan graduated from USC, he got hired by Veolia in San Diego. Sure, it was inaccurate to blame Dylan for being more successful, but it also seemed unfair that Dylan's bigger achievements had always impressed Dad more.

I sat up. This was pointless. I waded back into the water; it felt good against my sunbaked skin, and my muscles fell into their remembered rhythm.

I was hoping the swim back would clear my head, but instead it dredged up other thoughts. I still hadn't told Dylan about Leslie and me. Granted, he and I hadn't shared much of our personal lives over the past ten years, but Leslie and I *had* been engaged...

Focus on your breathing. Breathing. Yoga. Leslie had been good at yoga. *Hell.*

I knew that no matter how long I lived and how "whole" I eventually became, I would never be able to forget the first time I met Leslie. It was one of the memories I wanted to keep, despite the ache that came with it.

Leslie had come riding down the street in a green dress, her hair flowing like a sunburst of brown and gold around her face. She parked her bike in front of the cafe, and I decided I was better off studying at Linnaea's rather than meeting up with my study group over at Kreuzberg. She ordered a soy chai latte and I wanted to order something equally hip and organic, but all I could think of was how her honey-colored hands moved when she told the barista about her Cocker Spaniel and how her lips formed each word with such love.

She passed me with a smile, and my brain seized up and I didn't know what to do. So I ordered black coffee, which I never drank, and a day-old scone. I seated myself a couple of tables away from her and pulled one of my textbooks out of my backpack at random. Great. Physics. Now she would think I was a freshman or something, just because I'd left a GE class till my last quarter.

As I sat there, drawing cubes in my notebook instead of solving for buoyancy, I ran through possible scenarios. The most obvious solution was to walk over there, introduce myself, and ask her out. But that was *so* obvious. And terrifying. I needed a smoother approach. Ask her if she knew the internet password? I glanced furtively at her. No computer. She was reading a book – of *course* – because she was perfect. I could pretend to want to know the price of the artwork on the wall above her? Could work – but what if she made some comment about the medium the artist had used and I couldn't respond because I knew almost nothing about art? I tried to swallow another bite of scone, but it stuck in the back of my throat and I had to take a swig of coffee, which was so strong that it made my eyes water.

I looked around for my napkin, but it had disappeared at this critical juncture, just as my nose began to run. I was getting ready for an inconspicuous sprint to the bathroom when I felt a tap on my shoulder. She stood, laughing down at me, holding out a napkin.

"I'm here to ingratiate myself by any means necessary, in hopes of convincing you to help me with my physics homework."

I stared up at her, my nose buried in the napkin. There were several beats before I remembered to say yes, I *would* be happy to help her. By this point, she was no doubt regretting that she had chosen me as her physics tutor. Couldn't maintain basic hygiene, couldn't handle a conversation with a girl ...But I wasn't about to let her bail.

I coughed a final cough. "So. What section are you in?"

"8 a.m. Monday, Wednesday, Friday." She made a face: "For my sins."

"11:30, Tuesday, Thursday. And I'm Jim, by the way." I offered my hand.

"Leslie." She gave me one of her slow smiles.

When she smiled, I realized that her eyes were green, that she was still holding my hand and that I was barely breathing, all at the same time.

When I got back to the sailboat, Dylan had just hauled himself over the other side, his ditty bag heavy with two or three large sea bass. I offered to clean them as a kind of peace offering – and also because I didn't want to feel I had contributed nothing to our first meal in which we were actually "living off the ocean." I filleted the fish, reminding myself of the times I'd watched Dad and Uncle Ernie do the same thing. Run the knife from tail to gills along either side of the spine, separating the meat from the bones, and be careful not to puncture the bulging purple gut.

Dylan reemerged from the cabin a bit later, a frying pan in one hand. "Thanks for cleaning the fish." He picked up the pile of pink flesh.

"Sure," I said to his back.

That evening, Dylan made margaritas – because he was good at it and we needed a conversational lubricant – and we sat on the deck, watching the sun journey towards the limitless blue of the horizon. The silence between us was rendered more profound by the soft lapping of the waves against *Nelly*'s hull. The Pacific was living up to its name.

"Remember that time we saw the green flash?" Dylan said after several minutes of nothing but the slap of water against the hull and rattle of ice cubes on plastic.

I took a generous swallow from my Dixie cup. "I didn't see it when you and Dad did, remember? I was driving and I looked over too late, because you guys didn't bother mentioning that it was a good night for a green flash."

Dylan shrugged: "Guess we thought, who'd be watching the road when they could be looking at the ocean? Anyway, you've seen one by now, right?"

"At that restaurant right on the water in La Jolla – the night after we came to see your new place, I think." I tried not to think too much about that "we." "I remember the restaurant got really quiet as the sun went down, and everyone was staring at the sun. The last sliver disappeared, and there was a green glow on the horizon, and everyone in the room started clapping." I snorted. Applause had seemed a wholly insufficient response.

"I wonder if we'll see anything tonight," Dylan said, nodding toward the bronzing sky.

"It's clear enough."

That would seem like a sort of benediction on our trip if we saw a green flash. Like Noah and his rainbow. But the last mandarin section of sun slipped below the water and nothing happened. Well, "nothing" is the wrong word. The sky still blazed its final, dying glory, turning the mountains and farthest corners of the compass a breathy pink.

I stared at the darkening water where it licked at the boat and took a last sip, my tongue finding a few remaining grains of salt on the rim: "Well, that was good, but how about some dinner?"

Dylan nodded.

"You know, if that Veolia thing doesn't work out for you, there's always bartending."

He punched my arm, hard.

The next morning I was headachy, and Dylan wasn't far behind, judging by his bitter stare at the cereal box. We'd followed dinner with more margaritas, PBR, and any other beer that was lying around. I'm not really sure why, but drinking seemed the thing to do. Maybe it was the first time we'd felt at home enough on the boat to realize what – who – was missing. Now we slouched around, united in our hostility towards life.

Dylan first spoke about an hour after we got up: "Wanna go find some waves? They were saying something on the radio earlier about a big swell coming in. I've heard there's a spot just south of here where the surf's pretty good – when there are any waves at all."

I poured myself more coffee. "I haven't surfed in years."

"Don't worry, it'll come back to you. Like riding a bike – except, completely different."

I grinned a little. Why *had* it been so long since I'd done something I loved so much? In college, I'd as soon surf as eat – although I usually came out of the water as hungry as a shark. Some evenings I'd stay in the water till the final flush of sunset was gone from the sky, till there was no one on the beach, till the only way to see at all was to surf within range of the lights on the pier. The freedom of the cold water, the inner rush as I flung myself onto my board and started to paddle; then, sitting outside and waiting for the next set to come in, and seeing the mountains, the cliffs, the beach, the crummy beach town as if I'd never seen them before. A gull would swoop low or a curious seal would pop up next to me or a pair of dolphins would jump, and I'd be at peace with the world again. Why on earth did I quit?

"I didn't bring a board."

"No worries. I brought an extra," Dylan said.

"Can we anchor nearby, or – "

"Seriously, Jim: relax. I've got it covered."

By the time we moored *Nelly* in her new spot, it was early afternoon. "No point going out right now," Dylan said. "Surfing will be shitty, with the tide as it is. Let's take a nap and then go."

Waking up in the late afternoon heat was disorienting, but the best thing about naps is getting a second chance at the day. It felt weird to be wearing only a spring suit to go surfing – I had to keep reminding myself that the water was warmer here. Still, the weight of the board and the heavy, sweet coconut smell of the wax were pleasantly familiar. We paddled ashore and followed directions Dylan had gotten from a surfer he'd talked to back in Ensenada. I shifted my board from one arm to the other. Dylan had given me Dad's old board, which had seemed like a nice gesture until I realized how far we were going to be carrying our boards, and that Dad's was feet longer than Dylan's.

Finally, we rounded a bend and the dirt track dumped us out on a lonely curve of beach. The sand was grey-white and coarse, and the break was *big*. I watched a set come in, waves peeling to left and right.

Dylan gave a whoop and plunged into the surf. I followed, devoutly hoping I wouldn't eat it the entire time. I looked at the jade water sudsing around my ankles. Probably warm enough for stingrays – better shuffle. I didn't have much time for thinking or shuffling though, because a wave broke right on top of me, long before I'd made it out past the whitewater, and I got sucked under. The wave took me, forced me into a somersault, and held me down long enough to make my heart rate jump. I flailed for the surface. It was hard to find for a minute. When at last I emerged, gasping for air, it was just in in time to see the next wave coming. I grabbed for Dad's board and managed not to fall over as the wave broke. My mouth tasted like I'd just eaten a spoonful of salt. I threw myself forward onto my board and paddled hard.

It took a couple of attempts, but I finally made it out to where Dylan sat, rolling with the swells, his face toward the horizon as he watched for the next set.

"Glad you could join us."

"Hey, I told you it's been a while – and some of these have got to be ten-footers."

"I wouldn't say double overheads. Maybe eight feet or so, with a few standouts." Dylan talked like a surf report.

I didn't bother arguing. Now that we were out here, I felt that remembered rush of calm – interrupted by a boost of adrenaline whenever I saw a wave that looked like it wanted to break too early. We bobbed for a couple of minutes with nothing but the break and a few hungry gulls to interrupt the quiet. Then the next set rolled in.

"Here we go!" Dylan shouted.

"You get this one."

I watched Dylan's board angle toward the shore, watched Dylan paddle like he was an Olympic swimmer in his final sprint, watched as the board and the wave caught and bonded.

Dylan whooped as he stood, he and his board racing out of my line of sight. Just in time, I turned to look at the swell. The next wave would be a good one, too. My breathing quickened. Then, as I swung my board around, memory locked in. By the time I was in the wave, I forgot to worry about when to stand and when to turn. The power of the water hurtled me forward, and I could hear the rush of the wave building behind me. I crouched and I was in the barrel. My hand skimmed the wall of water to my right; for a moment the whole world was suspended and at rest. Then I realized that I wasn't going to make it out before the wave folded over me completely, and I reverted to present-day Jim, who hated getting water up his nose, which of course I proceeded to do.

"Dude, nice one! Saw you get barreled! Did you make it out?"

I rolled my eyes. I was still panting from the fight to make it back outside.

Dylan grinned: "Don't worry – plenty more where that came from!" He turned his board and paddled out again.

I sat bobbing on my board, trying to slow my breathing and spit out as much of the salt taste as I could. I thought about the first time Dylan and I had gone boogie boarding with our cousins. We came home, excited to tell Dad all about it. Dad snorted, threw his long board on the roof of the Volvo, and took us back down to Pismo Beach so we could see how *real* Californians rode waves. Watching Dad catch a wave for the first time, I thought he was probably the best surfer in the state – maybe the world. Dylan kept shouting that he wanted to try it. We were both surprised when we couldn't stand up the first time.

We surfed through the golden light of sunset and into its rosy afterglow. Pelicans and gulls became moving silhouettes above the horizon. The evening star appeared in the gathering dark. When the lesser stars began to show up, Dylan and I propped our boards against a bleached log and sprawled out on the beach. The surface of the sand had already lost its heat, but when I burrowed down, a little warmth remained in the moist sand underneath. I laid back and scooped sand over me, spring suit and all.

I turned my head to look at Dylan. Dylan's eyes were wide, taking in the blossoming constellations of the night sky. We lay there in silence. Then my stomach gurgled.

Dylan turned his head: "*¿Tienes hambre?*"

"*¿Cómo se dice* 'starving'?"

"Well, since we didn't go fishing today, how about some rice and beans?"

"I was thinking steak, but there probably aren't any wild cattle around here to slaughter, so beans work too."

By the time we'd made it back to the boat, the serenity of the ocean had worn off – for me, anyway. While we waited for the rice to cook, Dylan uncorked a bottle of rosé that must have been on the boat when Dad bought it, but I told myself wasn't *that* desperate for a drink. I could wait till we picked up some more beer at our next port.

Dylan proffered the bottle again when he went for his second glass.

"No thanks."

I watched the pink legs slowly form and slip back as Dylan swirled his glass. My mouth felt dry. I wondered again if alcoholism really was written into some people's genes. "Everyone likes a good tipple," an old friend of my dad's used to say. He was from the UK. Or was it Australia?

Dylan stirred the pan of bubbling beans. I thought maybe his silence had a different quality to the usual. We hadn't talked about Dad's death since the voyage began. We barely talked about Dad at all, which some might find odd, considering this whole trip had been his idea. I had a feeling we should talk about him – like, really talk about him – equal only to my wish never to talk about such things to another living soul.

I turned to hunt for salsa in the hobbit-sized pantry. I was the older brother – presumably that meant I had the lion's share of maturity. Should I be the one...? I heard the bottle pour again.

I returned with a jar of Pace and set it heavily on the counter. That mature conversation could wait.

"Jim. Jim? Jim!"

I heard something launch through the air and felt the *thunk* as it made contact with my skull.

"Ouch! What did you just throw at me?" I struggled to a sitting position in my bunk – we had yet to transition to sleeping above decks.

"Tolstoy. *Anna Karenina*, to be specific."

"*Why?*"

"You're wasting resources."

I assumed he meant my reading light. I switched it off. "Happy?"

"Getting there. What book 're you pretending to read?"

I felt around my sleeping bag for my book, its pages so well-fingered they felt like fabric. "One of the best books of all time."

"That's why you were snoring, obviously."

I aimed and threw.

"Ow."

"You're welcome. Pain builds character. So does Hemingway."

"No shit."

"Show a little respect. He was one of Dad's favorites."

Dylan peered at the orange back cover by the dim light still shining above his head. "How is it?"

"Great. Just finished it actually, and was resting from my labors when I was assaulted."

Dylan shrugged. He went back to turning the book over in his hands. "What's it about?"

"A guy and a girl."

"What else is new?"

"But they can never be together."

Dylan snorted: "Why not?"

"You should read the book."

"I probably will. But why not?"

"Because of an injury he got during World War I."

"So... she's a superficial bitch?"

"Not exactly. I mean, they *physically* can't be together." I couldn't say it – not to Dylan. He was still my baby brother.

"Like – "

"Yeah."

"Damn." A pause. "That's all it's about?" Dylan said.

"No. There's bullfighting – fishing – a boxer – Pamplona – Paris..."

"So why didn't you say that first?"

"Because that's all secondary."

"In your opinion."

"Yes," I said.

Dylan flipped the book open to the flyleaf. "'To Shelley, love Dave.'" He dropped it on the floor.

"What?"

Dylan put on a casual face: "Dad gave that to *Mom*...?"

"Yeah."

Dylan picked the book back up. Flipping far into it this time, he read: "'There were so many people running ahead of the bulls that the mass thickened and slowed up going through the gate into the ring, and as the bulls passed, galloping together, heavy, muddy-sided, horns swinging, one shot ahead, caught a man in the running crowd in the back and lifted him into the air. Both the man's arms were by his sides, his head went back as the horn went in, and the bull lifted him and then dropped him.'"

I thought it sounded like a pretty good metaphor for life.

II.

I couldn't place my sense of discomfort immediately. As my brain woke up, I registered a yowling outside. I sat up and waited for what felt like vertigo to pass, but the cabin kept pitching back and forth. That was what I was feeling – sick to my stomach.

Dylan moaned from the other side of the cabin: "Today's gonna blow."

A weather prediction as well as a qualitative assessment.

"Let's get out of here." I already had one foot on the companionway. If I stayed below any longer, I'd lose last night's dinner, at the very least.

As soon as my face reached the fresh air, wind caught at me with invisible claws. I pulled myself up and, leaning into the wind, made my way to the helm. My t-shirt flapped against me, as if to fly away.

I looked out to sea: white caps coated the water like a dusting of snow. Good thing we were already safely anchored. The discomfort we were experiencing here, in the relative shelter of the cove, was nothing to what it would have been out there; seasickness would have been the least of our worries. I looked to the lee. Dust smudged everything shoreward, making the *pueblo* that lay inland float above the desert like a mirage.

Dylan came up looking as green as I'd felt minutes before. I thought about teasing him, but I didn't feel confident enough yet. Dylan's mouth moved, but none of his words made it through the wind. I shook my head.

"Let's get out of here," he yelled in my face.

A few minutes later we were bumping across our little bay in the dinghy, skipping over the swells toward the closest bit of land with a visible road. Dylan had to turn his Padres cap backward to keep it from flying off. I tasted salt every time I licked my chapping lips.

We stashed the dinghy above high tide line among some rocks, where we figured it wouldn't be seen. No one would be coming to this little beach today, anyway.

I hoisted my empty pack onto my shoulder and started walking. This weather put me in a mood. Sand clung to my lips now along with the salt, and the only thing keeping me going was the thought of an ice cold Pacifico with a wedge of lime in some *cantina* where the wind was *not*.

Dylan jogged past me up the road and stuck out his thumb. He'd sure bounced back from his recent malaise. When I reached him, he was *whistling*. I took a step or two back and the wind carried the sound away. He looked dangerously close to breaking into song – probably something like "Bringing Sexy Back," judging from the snatches of tune I'd had inflicted on me – when a car appeared in the distance. Dylan stopped whistling and waited as the car disappeared into a dip in the road, then reemerged close at hand.

The sleek black Land Rover was coated in dust, but the license plate as it flashed by without slowing was Californian. I blew out a breath – a moment before I'd had the unpleasant sensation that we were about to be picked up by Mexican drug lords. They didn't really operate here much though, did they? Wasn't that the mainland? Add it to the list of things we should have checked before sailing...

We stood there, the wind gusting at us, Dylan close enough that I could hear him singing Justin Timberlake. I gritted my teeth and wished for a cup of coffee (or better, something stronger) and a few hours of solitude.

Another car whipped by in the opposite direction. Then, a stuttering red truck pulled over and the driver waved us into the back. A couple of men already sat there, faces half-shaded by hats or hoodies, apparently indifferent alike to the weather and the advent of two more bodies to share the small truck bed.

The car struggled on again, a jet of inky smoke lingering in our wake.

The road to town was unpaved. Endless tires gnawing away at the dirt had created corduroy that kept our teeth rattling. The dust from the road mingled with the dust already stirred up by the wind. I watched the landscape to distract myself from an overpowering smell of exhaust.

Scruffy manzanitas, century plants, and yucca grew in patches across the flat terrain, which was broken now and then by stunted hills. The soil looked like it came from Mars; that burnt orange belonged to an alien planet. At last the town began to materialize around us by way of a large Tecate sign, a gas station, and then a smattering of trailers and low houses. The truck swung right onto the paved main road, and we careened to the left and came to rest a short time later in the pitted lot outside a store with "Cerveza, Refrescos, Coca Cola" on a handwritten sign in the window. The truck shut off, but the Mariachi band on the radio kept playing. Then the driver got out and the music shut off. All that was left was the wind. The silent men got out of the truck bed one by one.

"*Gracias,*" said Dylan, jumping down and offering the driver a pack of cigarettes. I frowned. Dylan caught my look and shrugged.

"*De nada,*" the man smiled as he pocketed the pack.

"*Buscamos – por la cantina,*" Dylan said, raising his voice against the wind.

"*Oh, sí.*" He scratched his jaw. "*¿Cómo se dice en Inglés, derecho?*" He gestured along the main street: "*Derecho –* straight – *y entonces,*" he waved his left hand, "*izquierda. ¿Comprendes?*" He looked at Dylan, not optimistic.

Dylan nodded.

"*Gracias,*" I said. The word sounded so flat in my throat. My "r" had none of the rounded warmth of this language I'd spent so much of my life listening to. If the color of a language were an index of life, what did that mean for modern English speakers and our abbreviated, homogenized vocabulary?

We walked quickly down the main street. It was still morning, but it felt like it had been blowing for days.

I rotated my face just far enough for Dylan to catch my voice: "Why did you bring cigarettes? I thought you quit."

"Thanks for the concern, big brother, but I can take care of myself now."

"Fine. But do you have to spread – "

"My filthy habit? He didn't have to take them. And it's not like I was giving him *Playboy* or anything."

I watched a vulture soar over the road on his way toward the desert. Words I wanted to say tasted like bile as I swallowed them back.

We walked into the *cantina*. Early as it was, we were not the first ones there. A lone figure hunched at the counter. Four Americans sat at a table off to the right. You could tell they were new to Baja from the way they carried themselves: boisterous, yet sticking close together, eyes a little too wide.

Dylan and I ordered Pacificos and some chips and salsa. Dylan leaned back against the counter, beer in hand, an easy allusion to Paul Newman in *Butch Cassidy and the Sundance Kid*. "Want to find a table?"

I knew what he was thinking. "Before you go over there, think about the fact that there are two guys and two girls."

"Who says –"

"So you don't want to talk to the *gringos*?"

"Tell me you don't crave a little attention from the fairer sex yourself."

"Whatever. Just don't start laying on the charm too thick or we're out of here."

Dylan collected the chips and salsa and made his way to a table right next to the four of them. I shook my head, paid the man behind the counter, and slowly walked over to join my brother. I wondered why I hadn't put up more of a fight. It was within the realm of possibility that my lack of resistance had something to do with the cutoffs and barely concealed bikini tops at the table to which Dylan was already pulling up a chair.

"Oh hey, guys, this is my older brother, Jim."

We swapped *heys* and Dylan rattled off names like he'd known them his whole life: "Billy, Kim, Hailey, Traven."

I nodded, already forgetting which names and faces went together.

"Dylan says you taught yourself to navigate?" The blonde girl – Kim? – turned her well-outlined eyes on me.

"Is it hard?" said the brunette girl... dammit, what was her name?

"Well – " I blinked.

"Very," Dylan said, "because we're sailing by the stars.

"Wow," the girls chorused.

"So you know a lot of good fishing spots?" said the bigger of the two guys, his thick lips curling in a smile. A chunky gold ring featuring one massive ruby flashed as he ran a hand through his fair hair.

I hesitated, then nodded: "Mmm." I took a swig of beer and studied the brown bottle with its yellow label.

Dylan frowned at me and stepped in: "Well, we haven't been here that long yet."

The blond guy smiled again: "You guys will have to give me some tips – we've got to catch fish soon, or the girls are threatening to mutiny."

One of the girls flipped her hair and laughed. The other played with her big hoop earrings. The better part of me knew they were crafting each response, but I still felt myself weakening.

"Well, yeah – we found a pretty good bass hole not far from where we're anchored, if you like bass," I said.

The other guy spoke up for the first time since I'd sat down: "Have you guys caught many lobster?" This guy – Traven, possibly – was the direct inverse of his friend: his brown hair fell in waves to his shoulders, and his pale face was narrow as a ferret's.

We had yet to catch a single lobster. It was Dylan's turn to hesitate.

"We're not super experienced at free diving yet – and that's the main way we'd catch them," I said.

Our new acquaintances looked like I'd told them Jay-Z and Beyoncé had broken up.

"Although," I added, "I did notice some lobster traps when we were coming in this morning, so there's bound to be lobster around."

Everyone cheered up at this and Dylan ordered a round of *cervesas* for the table. Bottle caps popped with a satisfying sound, and a citrus smell hung in the air from the lime wedges we pushed into our bottles.

"Ooh, yum!" exclaimed the girl who was probably not Kim. Apparently, this was her first Pacifico.

"So what brings you down here?" I asked.

"You mean, like, business or pleasure? Business, definitely," said the blond guy, smirking. Everyone laughed.

"But where are you headed?"

"Don't know, man, the girls are saying Cabo, but we're kinda just road trippin' it. See what happens, you know?"

Dylan bobbed his head: "I feel you, man. We want to get to Panama and back before the hurricane season, but I'm really digging the chance to explore Baja on the way."

This was the first time I'd heard Dylan describe our trip to anyone.

"Panama?! Hailey and I were just talking about how we've never been there!" said Kim.

I wondered whether this had actually been a subject of discussion. I nodded anyway.

The wind blew on and more rounds were ordered, and the pale guy offered us molly ("Haha, I can't take him anywhere," laughed the big guy), and Kim asked the big guy – whom she addressed as Billy – to come outside for a reefer. She looked at Dylan too, though not at me. Dylan might have gone for one, but Hailey was leaning in towards him – a hand on either shoulder – debating the finer points of French kissing. Dylan wasn't going anywhere.

I went to the men's room and found Traven standing in front of the sink, staring at the flowing tap.

I turned off the faucet: "Dammit, man, haven't you heard you're in the middle of a desert?"

I got no response, just a stare like a child's when you've taken his lollypop. When I came back out – alone, as Traven was busy poking his reflection in the discolored mirror – I found Dylan telling Billy to rent a boat tomorrow and we would show them where to go for the best fishing. Well, at least he wasn't volunteering to take them out in *Nelly*.

"Think there are any places around here that rent boats, though? Talk about nowheresville."

"For the right price? Sure."

"Of course," Billy rubbed his thumb against his index and middle fingers. "*Di-ner-o.* Gotta sweeten the deal."

'Vulgar' was the word that came to mind as I watched him. And it wasn't a word I had used before to describe a person of my acquaintance.

"So where do you want to meet tomorrow?"

Dylan and Billy dove into practicalities, and I found myself sitting between a drunk brunette and a blonde pothead. Still, they were two of the most attractive specimens of substance abuse that I had met with.

"What if it's still blowing tomorrow?" I asked Dylan as we hitchhiked back to the spot where we'd left the zodiac.

The other four were staying in town for the night, and we had politely refused a ride from Billy, who'd offered to drive us, reefer in hand. We had to do some grocery shopping, as I'd reminded Dylan.

"It won't be."

"But what if it is?" I wobbled a little as I walked forward to stick out a thumb.

Thankfully, Dylan didn't notice; he had a prophetic gleam in his eye: "Wait and see. Hot and glassy – I promise."

The wind went down with the sun, and we ventured below decks to cook a late dinner.

"Nice to have some company today," Dylan said.

"Yeah."

"I don't think they're all dating each other."

I shot Dylan a glance: "Wait, so this fishing trip isn't all high-minded altruism?"

"That's one quality I'm not often accused of." Dylan grinned: "C'mon, I saw you looking smug with them leaning in on either side of you."

I looked down at the (scorching) pot of refried beans I was supposed to be watching to hide a smile. For about two seconds it felt like things were back to normal.

I should probably tell him about Leslie.

I climbed up on deck and caught my breath. The sun slanted at the bay from over the distant hills, and the water reflected the sun's warmth back in pearly pinks, blues and grays. A light breeze kept it cool, but it was still early, so that would change soon. Hot and glassy. How did Dylan do it?

"Good morning!" Dylan emerged with two cups of earthy black coffee.

"Well, I see you're finally taking your responsibilities as the younger brother seriously," I reached for a mug.

"Let's just say I know which side my bread is buttered on," Dylan said, holding the coffee out of reach. "The question is, do you?"

"Fine, I'll play nice today," I said.

"Good." Dylan relinquished the cup.

I took a life-giving sip. "They coming to us or what?"

"No."

"No?"

"They're picking us up from the road in an hour and we're driving back up to that bigger town with the marina. I figure it makes sense, since the bass hole is back that way."

"They should just come here with the boat."

"Well I can't call and tell them that now. This is how we set it up, so this is how it's gonna be. Anyway, they'll need help choosing a boat."

I stared out at the perfect conditions: "By the time we get out there, there won't be any fish left."

"Drink your coffee, Jim."

Somehow, by the time we made it to the rendezvous point, a little over an hour had elapsed. No car was in sight.

"Maybe they gave up on us," Dylan said, walking out into the road and looking in both directions.

"No, they're just late." *I could have told you this would happen*, I added to myself.

"You think?" Dylan ruffled up his hair.

"I think you should get out of the middle of the road, for starters."

Sure enough, five minutes later, a car flashed into sight. I had a moment of déjà vu as a black Land Rover sailed by. Then the brakes squealed, infusing the morning air with the scent of burning rubber. The SUV skidded to a dusty stop in front of us. Billy & Co. were dressed in stylishly ineffectual fishing attire.

"Good morning," Billy boomed, several decibels louder than necessary.

I nodded and began loading our tackle into the back of the Land Rover while Dylan and Hailey exchanged a very friendly good morning.

By the time we were on the road, the rest of us had thawed out a little, and by the time the boat had been selected, we were discussing politics. I like to think of topics of conversation as a barometer for how comfortable people feel around each other. Politics is above alcohol and music preferences, but below personal history and religion.

"Dude, universal healthcare is such a scam. We'll be paying for so many illegals, we won't have any resources left to treat our own citizens." Billy rested his free hand on Kim's thigh. "Grab me a cold one, okay?"

She leaned down to the cooler at her feet, but she didn't look too happy about it. I had to agree with her.

And – what the hell? Here he was, a trust fund baby, complaining about providing healthcare to illegal immigrants who were sick enough to risk deportation to see a doctor. Forget the fact that our economy benefited hugely from the manual labor they provided. I tried to catch Dylan's eye, but he seemed preoccupied with Hailey, who "had" to have him help her reapply sunscreen as soon as they were aboard the boat. Traven sat by himself. I wasn't sure if he was tripping balls or what.

The first hitch came with the question of who should drive the boat. Initially, I'd thought one of the four of them could handle it – with some direction from Dylan or myself. But given that Billy's only specification was that they wanted "a big motor boat," I was now far from convinced.

I headed for the wheel almost by instinct once we were all aboard, but I came head to head with Billy on my way there. Billy *had* paid for the vessel, but he hadn't bought life insurance for its occupants.

Dylan spoke up: "Maybe Jim should steer us out of here – these waters can be treacherous if you're not familiar with the area."

That was the first I'd heard of "these treacherous waters," but I was grateful for any reason to delay surrendering a high-powered piece of machinery into hands as green as Billy's. As I took us out of the marina, Dylan explained the concept of steering loudly to Hailey, who seemed pleasingly unaware that this explanation wasn't solely for her benefit.

The boat purred into the bay. The bow sliced through the water like scissors through silk. A seagull or two circled speculatively, and the sun beat down on us, made bearable only by the wind we created as we sped over the water. When we were nearly in the crosshairs of our landmarks for the bass hole, I cut the engine and we drifted, a hint of diesel mingling with the tang of the waves. We rocked gently, and for a few seconds all was perfect calm. Then Billy emerged from the ice chest, a beer in each fist:

"Let's kill some fish, *biatches*!"

Hailey clapped, Kim woo-hooed – even Dylan smiled. I refrained from an eye roll. Traven seemed the only one unaffected by Billy's entrance, most likely because he was getting sick over the side.

Dylan started giving a tutorial on casting. He released the catch and, in time with a fluid motion of his arm, let the line swirl away from under his thumb. Then, when the line stopped moving and before it could snag on the bottom, he began to reel: steadily, slowly, with little tugs and variations in speed to attract the fish to his lure. I could hear Uncle Ernie and Dad's voices in my head, explaining the technique. There was a long, intervening silence. Nothing happened, so Dylan cast again.

This time, as the line flitted back toward the boat, there was a twitch, then a jerk. Hailey bobbed up and down with little cries of excitement.

"Who wants to bring him in?" Dylan said.

Billy's hands closed around the pole.

Unlike Dad and Uncle Ernie, Dylan's voice stayed at a conversational level as he showed Billy how to keep the right amount of resistance going between him and the fish, told him – multiple times – not to let the pole touch the side of the boat, and watched as all of his instructions were ignored and the fish lost.

"Son of a bitch!"

"I think you're getting the hang of it. Try casting." Dylan reached for another pole: "Who else wants to try?"

Of course Hailey did, and of course I got to unsnag Billy from the bottom. But in between cursing the rod, the fish, the boat, and everyone in it, Billy seemed to be making an effort to be likeable. I just wasn't sure if it was working out for him. He was clearly used to being liked, however, and I watched with amusement as he tested out different tacks to engage me in a conversation where he could exert the full force of his charm.

"No, man, I think Machiavelli's onto something," Billy looked around to make sure no one else was listening. We were on philosophy now. "Love gets you nowhere, dude."

I watched Billy's eyes locate Kim, who had found a scrap of deck where she could lay out.

"Well, I'll give you that, for the sake of argument."

I saw Dylan's hands over Hailey's, drawing the pole back for a cast. She twisted toward him to say something and Dylan leaned in for a kiss. I looked away. Not that you ever want to see your brother kissing a girl, but at this particular moment the contrast between us seemed to have reached a point of farce. Dylan makes out with hot girl while Jim talks 10th grade philosophy with a capital-A asshole.

Perhaps sensing my inattention, Billy drifted from the topic, but I prodded him back: "Well, I'm pretty sure real love is a lot less common than we think," I said. "And anyway, I'm pretty sure Machiavelli wasn't talking about romantic love at all."

"Well," Billy chewed his cheek as he cast his line yet again, "the principle is the same – " he stopped. "Dude, I've got one!"

"Okay, nice and steady. Keep your pole up – no, pole *up!*" I struggled to bring my voice back to a polite level. "Keep reeling!"

Billy reeled, his forehead pearling with sweat. It was hot now that we didn't have the wind from the motion of the boat to cool us.

"Okay, now, when you can see the fish, lift the rod – no. Stop reeling. Lift the *rod* so I can get him with the net. Right. Dylan, do you have the pl – damn!"

"What?" Dylan and Billy spoke together, and Kim raised herself on one elbow.

Even Traven's face miraculously appeared, looking less green, if no less high.

"Oh damn," said Dylan, passing me the pliers.

"What the hell's wrong?" Billy shouted.

I exhaled. "It's a corvina – it's on the list of banned fish."

"So...?"

"So we'll have to throw it back," I said.

"Are you shitting me?"

"No." Dylan shook his head. "If a patrol boat came by and found us with that fish, it would be a big fine and even bigger hassle. Too bad, that's a decent sized one – probably at least four pounds."

I began to remove the hook from the tender flesh of the gill. The fish twitched.

Billy recovered from momentary speechlessness.

"Come on guys – my *first catch*!"

"Hey, it was a good one, even if you can't keep it," said Dylan.

"Yeah, at least it's not too small – that's usually the reason we'd throw a fish back. This one's the real deal." I smiled, but Billy wasn't smiling back.

"Does Mexico even *have* a fish and game department? No one's going to know!"

No one else spoke.

"Look – you talked me into renting this damn boat. I'll put it at the bottom of the ice chest and cover it with ice and beers. One fish more or less isn't gonna make or break the ecosystem."

Dylan looked at me. The hair on the back of my neck prickled like a dog's, but this wasn't a hill to die on, so I shrugged and Dylan shrugged and let Billy take the fish. Silence followed. Everyone became preoccupied with whatever they were doing till Hailey's line – and Hailey – jumped.

I breathed more easily when she had reeled in and it was a bass. The fishing was far better than I had predicted, and by the time no one could go any longer without taking a break for food, we had pulled in more than we could conceivably eat over the next few days. We sat down and opened some more beers, then I pulled out the equipment for PB and J. Kim, who had been content to watch other people catch fish while ensuring that her skin browned evenly, got up to help. I slapped peanut butter on one slice of bread and she slathered strawberry jam on another and pressed the two together.

Dylan and the others, meanwhile, continued to rest from their labors and drink beer. I was surprised to find I didn't mind. I said something vaguely funny and Kim laughed. She brushed against me when she reached for the bread, and then again when she wanted another sip of beer. When the sandwiches were finished, she planted a blob of jam on the end of my nose. I retaliated with peanut butter. Somehow this devolved into a silent tickling match that ended with us facing each other, a little breathless, my hands locked around her wrists. I didn't even realize I was leaning in until I heard a laugh and glanced behind me.

All eyes were on us. I looked away from Dylan's (mocking) eyes only to run into Billy's. He shrugged. Traven went on staring without apparent embarrassment, and Hailey giggled again. The blood rushed to my face and I released Kim's wrists. I didn't even know her. Worse, I had been thinking, just a few hours ago, that she was about as one-dimensional as they came.

Kim pouted her lips at me for a moment, then returned to sunning herself. I put the peanut butter and jam away feeling foolish. What was most irritating was the suspicion that I ought to have kissed the girl if I was going to get laughed at either way.

Billy finished off his sandwich and tossed his empty bottle over the side. "All right! Let's catch some more fish!"

"Whoa!" Dylan fished the bottle out with the net while Billy cocked his head to one side. Dylan turned slowly, the net dripping on deck: "I think we have all we can eat for the next several days – any more and it will just go bad on us."

"But fishing is so much fun!" Hailey widened her eyes at Dylan.

"Nah, it's cool, dude," Billy said. "I've got this buddy who's gonna hook me up with a company that packs your fresh fish and flies it out from several locations in Baja – all I need is ice to keep the fillets cold for like a day."

My jaw dropped a little.

"But how much do you really *need*?" Dylan looked as if he was beginning to realize whom he was dealing with.

"Dude, chill! Don't get your panties in a wad. We can stop fishing. Let's go dive for some lobster." Billy turned to me: "Where did you say you saw those traps?"

I blinked.

Dylan had his Texas hold 'em face on, no emotion escaping from behind the mask. "Not sure how much we can help you with the lobster. Like I said, we haven't done a lot of diving yet."

"No worries, man. I've been snorkeling before. In the Bahamas. How different can it be?"

"Okay."

Dylan looked at me like I'd agreed to harpoon a dolphin.

"Damn straight! I had them fit us out with some gear at the marina, just in case. You guys have yours on your boat, right? We'll swing by for it, then we can catch some lobster!"

Hailey sidled over to Dylan, who still looked bewildered by my change of tone. I smiled. I had finally recognized with whom I was dealing. The brief fever-dream – Kim, to be precise, now practicing yoga in the sun – was over. These were The Rich. Hemingway had written about them fifty-plus years ago, but they had not changed. I remembered his words from *A Moveable Feast*: "The understanding rich... who give each day the quality of a festival and who, when they have passed and taken the nourishment they needed, leave everything deader than the roots of any grass Attila's horses' hooves have ever scoured."

Dylan kept casting me what-are-you-doing glances as we grabbed our snorkeling equipment and piloted our psyched / apathetic passengers to the inlet where I'd seen the most lobster traps.

"I've only watched my d – watched people lobster dive as a kid. So why don't I take one or two of you down to start with and then, if all goes well, we can see who else wants to go?" I said.

Weight belts. Masks. Mouthpieces. Fins. I looked at Billy and Kim, who had both suited up beside me. I pulled on a pair of gloves.

"I don't think they gave us any gloves..." Kim looked nervous.

I avoided eye contact with Dylan: "Don't worry about it – just let Billy and me grab them. I'm sure Billy won't have any trouble – his hands look tough enough."

Billy made the 'rock on' sign. I stared at his thick fingers, including the gold pinky ring, for a moment before I realized I needed to give the word.

"Okay, let's go!" I led the way over the side.

The water was so clear we could see our own shadows drifting like clouds below us. Sunlight slanted around us in prismed columns. There was no noise of motors, no conversation, no seagulls screaming, just a great hush like the night after a heavy snow. We swam like seals, the big fins propelling us far along with each kick. I glanced at a few empty lobster traps as we passed, making sure to avoid the kelp beds and leading the way toward the rocks where most of the traps were set. When I got there, I felt a moment's relief – not a lobster in sight from ten or fifteen feet above. Then I took a long breath and dove down.

The lobsters were hard to see at first. Their rusty backs melded with the porous, red-brown rock. Then my eyes began to recognize their shapes – tucked tails, spiny backs, antennaed heads. They were everywhere: blending in with seaweed, poking out of holes, even sitting there in the light as if sunning themselves.

Billy dove down to join me and let out an exultant gurgle. He took the 'tickle stick' Dylan had given him and began to tease a promising-looking one from its lair. We both had to resurface for breath, but Billy was soon back at work. I looked up; Kim was still trying to get down to us. I felt slightly guilty about taking those weights out of the belt I'd given her, but it was for her own good.

At last, the lobster emerged with a swish of antenna and legs. Billy had a knife out within seconds. I shook my head and mimed grabbing the lobster by its back, as I'd seen Dad do many years ago. Billy grabbed the lobster but drew his hand away again quickly. It was bleeding, and he clutched it with his good hand, sending bubbles up through his snorkel. The lobster darted back into his crevice. Billy looked at me, his eyes through the mask and the water looking like the eyes of my first bass. He pointed up. We rose to the surface, spewing water and air.

He yanked the snorkel away from his mouth: "You tree-hugging sonofabitch. Give me your gloves. Now."

"What?"

"*You knew* what that lobster would do to me! My hand!"

It was mangled.

"Yeah, you've got to be careful how you grab them."

"No shit, Sherlock! You knew this would happen before we got in the water. Well, guess what? I'm taking *your* gloves and getting my lobster anyway. You can hand them over, or I can rip them off – with my teeth, if I have to."

It wasn't a hard decision. Billy could easily have drowned me – not that he wanted to, but it wasn't clear that he *didn't* want to. I am no hero, so I swam back to the boat, where Kim was already drying off.

She turned to look at me: "Where are your gloves?"

"Billy decided he needed them, after all."

Dylan looked over.

Kim frowned. Damn, she was still pretty.

"How come you aren't catching them barehanded, like you said Billy could?"

I shrugged.

The latter half of the afternoon wasn't the pleasantest. Billy got back with three lobsters and announced that the four of them were done. When Hailey and Kim tried to argue, he used a knife to cut my glove off his right hand and showed them his swollen, lacerated palm and fingers. The toxin from the lobster spines was beginning to take effect.

"Damn! You want some ice for that? Looks like that bug got you good," Dylan said, his eyes carefully avoiding the part of the boat where I was.

"No thanks. You can pilot us back to the marina. We're heading south today."

"*Today?*"

"We're taking our catch and are outta here," Billy said.

He stared at Dylan like he could fillet him with his eyes. Kim looked confused. Traven was unfazed as ever. Only Hailey protested.

"Did you not hear me, Hailey?" Billy got four inches from her face and roared: "Your friends did this to me!"

He brandished his strawberry-red hand in front of her. She stepped back, eyes round and lips pale. I thought she was going to cry, until both of their voices began to rise.

Dylan looked at me finally. "Great job." He hovered on the balls of his feet, ready to strike if Billy convinced him it was necessary.

Hailey's voice crescendoed into hysteria. I listened to her litany, whenever Billy paused for breath: "...Always ruin everything... Big baby... Can't stand to see anyone having fun if you're not..."

Billy threw his hands up like he was doing the wave at a football game, then winced.

"Come on, babe. You'll be happy again in the next town." The term of endearment sounded like a body blow. "Next time just make sure it's not with a Mother Nature-loving *asshole*."

"What?" Hailey looked back at Dylan.

Dylan glanced at me.

"We don't believe in raping the seas," I said, my voice only half-filling the sudden stillness.

I hadn't really meant to say it out loud. *That* would go down well. Dylan pursed his lips and turned away.

"Raping?!" Kim whirled to face me. "Thanks *so much* for not coming to any snap judgments about us," she said.

She moved away, to stand next to Billy and Hailey.

"No, actually, it *wasn't* a snap judgment." I felt that smile that had always infuriated Leslie emerging. I couldn't help it – it was a natural response to idiocy. I hadn't used it that often with Leslie, and seldom intentionally, but –

Hailey was laying into Dylan. I'd better stop smiling.

"... All a lie. You and your brother can spend your time worrying about a few fish. I am going to *live*."

The sun was making us all a little melodramatic.

I prepared an inoffensive face for the lovely rich: "So, you'd like us to pilot you back to the marina?"

Hailey started to say no, but Billy interrupted: "Why not? You got us out here." I went to restart the engine, but he placed himself between me and the wheel: "What should I do about my hand?"

"Maybe some ice. Don't worry, it'll be fine in a week." I couldn't extract all the satisfaction from my voice. He loomed over me, drew a breath, and expelled it in my face. Stale beer and spliffs. I waited, trying to look as dignified as I could. After a minute, he let me by to the wheel.

Without a word, Dylan divided the fish into two coolers.

After we returned the boat and the rented equipment, Billy gave us a wide, cherubic smile: "Well, take it easy. We gotta split – gotta get that fish shipped off A.S.A.P. so we can head to Cabo."

At the mention of Cabo, both girls started screaming and hugging each other. I wondered if this was part of the show, or if they genuinely could shift moods like Dad taught me to shift gears in his truck. As soon as we'd stepped off the boat, their personalities seemed to meld back into one. I wasn't sure if that said more about them or me.

"Hey, hope you can carry your catch and your gear back to your boat okay!" Billy was all solicitude as he came back with the car. He had elected to leave his SUV with the local hotel's valet service ("You can't really trust these guys around nice stuff unless there's a monetary incentive").

Dylan and I both recoiled like he'd thrown an actual punch at last.

"Wait, we're not driving them back?" Traven's eyes struggled to focus on us or the dusty road stretching ahead.

Apparently not. On a more positive note, at least we hadn't taken Traven snorkeling – he would have drowned, no question.

"All right. Peace." Billy revved the engine, looking anything but peaceable.

"Bye," said Dylan, trying to catch Hailey's eye.

"You shouldn't talk to *rapists* like us, Dylan." She scorched us both with a glance.

"Hailey..."

"And I don't talk to guys with no *cojones*. Ya feel me, *Babe*?"

Billy started to reverse the car, then stopped. He leaned out the window, flipped us off with both hands and shouted: "I hope your boat gets caught in a storm and you never make it to Panama."

Then he spun the wheel and tore down the gravel road, leaving us in a cloud of dust.

"Well, that was –" I began.

"Don't talk to me, you son of a –"

I smirked: "I'm your brother. We have the same mother. You can't call me that."

Dylan was silent, but it wasn't a satisfying silence.

I moved to pick up the ice chest, my dive gear dangling around my neck or stuffed into the seat of my pants, but Dylan was there before me. We started walking out of town.

"You know, I've never met a person with such a gift for bringing out the worst in people." Dylan spoke like there was a bad taste in his mouth.

"I didn't make them greedy, rich – "

"No, but you didn't have to use the most offensive way possible to call them out, either. And why lump them all together, anyway?"

"You *knew* what I was doing when I told him not to wear gloves," I said.

"Yeah, my mistake. I should have known you wouldn't be smooth enough to make it look like an accident. But I mean – *rapists*? Really?"

"It's true!"

"So is a lot of stuff I've never found it necessary to say to you. Maybe *that* was my mistake."

"You weren't happy about their fishing ethics, either. If you hadn't been so distracted with that girl, you'd have been as mad as I was."

"Fishing ethics? You do realize what a pompous ass you sound like, don't you?"

Dylan picked up the pace and walked directly in front of me, his tramping feet throwing dust back in my face. I sucked a cottony breath through gritted teeth.

We weighed anchor from our little harbor the next morning without much regret and set our sights on Bahia Tortuga, Baja Sur. But first, a little detour was required for more supplies.

By unspoken agreement we sailed well past the town we'd visited the day before, to where the map told us we would find another small bay, with another *pueblo* nearby.

III.

"*Diez pesos, por favor.*"

I pulled coins and bills, a Kleenex, and a rubber lure from my pocket, fumbling for the right denominations.

"*Gracias, señor.*" The man passed me two Coke bottles, sweating in the heat from his hands.

"*Gracias. Adios.*"

I nodded and pushed through the door into the violent sunshine, stooping to pop the bottle caps off on the step. Then I hurried down the baked road to where Dylan was canvassing a small outdoor market for limes, cilantro and other staples. I handed him a Coke.

"Thanks."

"No problem."

I stared at the market, gearing myself up for bartering. Dylan treated it like a game; to me it was an unpleasant chore. Then my gaze caught on the fruit stand. Standing there, among the piles of apples, bananas, and mangoes, was a woman. Her skin was the color of the hills and her eyes flashed warmth as they met mine.

Before I could form a coherent thought, Dylan came into my line of sight, walking over to her with a bouquet of flowers. The bastard. I hesitated for a second, then my feet pulled me in the same direction.

"Oh, hey Jim." Dylan seemed oblivious to the fact that she and I were soul mates. "This is Raquel. Raquel, this is my older brother."

I smiled automatically and extended my hand, ignoring the way Dylan had lingered on the word "older."

Her fingers grasped mine: "Jim. Nice to meet you."

That means you have to say something back, I told myself. Time to impress. But all I could come up with was, "Nice to meet you, too."

She smiled a generous smile – dazzling white teeth and the corners of her eyes creasing like tissue paper.

Dylan was saying something about boats, but I didn't come back to the conversation in time to catch it. Dylan and Raquel were still smiling, though, so I smiled too.

"Wouldn't it be great to have another sailor aboard?" Dylan said to me. "Think about the extra sleep when we need to sail through the night, the extra help if it storms ..."

She put up both hands. "Whoa! Slow down. I *have* just met you."

"Well, let's fix that." Dylan nodded towards the nearby *cantina*. I had flashbacks to the last 'friends' we had made over *cerveza*.

"Don't you think it's a little early for that?" Raquel said.

"If you say so," Dylan shrugged.

"Well, today I do. Actually, I'm about to go to mass at the local *iglesia*. We're having a meal afterwards."

She looked from Dylan to me and back to Dylan. What did she want?

"Sounds like you've got it wired," I said. Stupid.

"Well, I have family just outside of town. I've been here a week now – I nearly left on Friday, but my cousin Rosaria convinced me to stay through the weekend. She has two little boys and she misses her girl time."

"Well, I'm glad she – " I began.

"Wait, it's Sunday?" Dylan said. He shifted his weight from one foot to the other. "Can we get in on that meal?"

"Of course! It's for anyone who comes to the service."

I waited for Dylan to make an excuse, as he always did when I used to invite him to church, but he said: "What do you say, Jim? Say our prayers, then get some local *comida*?"

"Okay."

The last time I had prayed, I'd been standing in the doorway of my apartment, praying that this was a nightmare and that I wasn't actually seeing Leslie, like Judas, betraying me with a kiss. It wasn't that I didn't believe in God anymore – more like I didn't want to. How could a loving God create a world where good things were given, only to be taken away? I didn't know – didn't think I wanted to know.

Maybe it started even before that, though – the slip slidin' away, Paul Simon style. To be honest, praying hadn't been a regular part of my life since my dad died.

We walked into the little building; it smelled, like old churches do, of damp earth and candle wax and the wine used for communion – a scent holier than ordinary red wine. Backless benches served as pews, their wood smoothed and darkened from years of sitting. Candles burned in front of a rough painting of the Virgin and Child in a niche in the wall, and at the far end – which wasn't that far away at all – the tiled floor rose one step to the small, white-draped altar. A *padre* shuffled around behind the altar, making preparations for the celebration of the Eucharist later in the service, I assumed. The silver cup and salver looked out of place in these humble surroundings. I sat next to Dylan, trying not to look around for Raquel. No doubt she was on his other side, engrossed. Dylan was the happy possessor of one of those personalities that command attention. Good looks didn't hurt either, but I was convinced there was something more – something unquantifiable but perhaps approximated by that old phrase 'animal magnetism.' I'd seen it in action before.

I told myself I wasn't looking for Raquel, but I did anyway. Finally I saw her, talking in quick, rhythmic Spanish to a gray-haired woman who could not have been five feet tall. I relaxed – in the event, too soon, since for some reason my brain insisted on taking me back to the last time I had been at a Catholic church service.

It was my cousin Lawrence's funeral, and Leslie had come with me, albeit unwillingly. She doesn't believe in organized religion, and Catholic churches above all give her the creeps. So she told me. She also said that the incense they used at the church she was dragged to as a child reminded her of afterbirth (her dad was a vet), and the endless standing, sitting and kneeling gave her a pain in her back.

But she came, with an appropriately subdued smile, on my arm, and we joined in the age-old words: "Pray for us sinners now and at the hour of our death" (that line always reminded me of T. S. Eliot, rather than the other way around) and, "Forgive us our trespasses as we forgive those who trespass…."

A nudge yanked me back. We were standing for the first hymn and Raquel had slipped into the empty place beside me. Her voice swelled with the unfamiliar cadences, and I hungered, unexpectedly, to know her history, told in her own slightly husky tones. But the cold that the tile threw back at me sucked me under again like one of those big waves from our recent surf session.

The formality of that funeral mass had provided the only logic to which I could tether my mind. Lawrence – Law – had been seventeen years old. You heard about the tragedy of young death, but witnessing it, being enveloped by it – it was almost unfathomable. Law's siblings got up and talked about their favorite memories of him. Then came his parents. Their tears were serene, but I wondered if that serenity welled up from inside or was just painted on for the day.

Dylan elbowed me from the other side and I jerked, about to stand. Just in time, I noticed that everyone was kneeling for prayers. There were no leather-padded cushions, so we knelt on the adobe tiles and the grouted grooves between them…

Death is like that, anyway – unfathomable. A pain with a black hole at its center, sucking you down if you stare at it too long. Some of us choose to think about the loved ones who are gone as little as possible, lest we be devoured.

At Law's funeral, I had no reason to suspect that another awaited me within a year's time. Who could imagine that the calloused hands folded over the gentle paunch of the man to my right would be carefully arranged by a mortician before another summer had reached its zenith? No, that day at the Mission I was rendered speechless by the pain of others more than my own, although I already missed my young cousin, with the aching knowledge that I would never get to know him as well as I wanted to. That is, I wasn't sure. The priest said we'd see Law again in a better world. But did you get to do things like cliff jumping in heaven? Because that's what Law had asked me to do with him. *Take me to Big Falls, Jim. Please! Dad won't let me take the Toyota out there.* And me: *July for sure. I've just got to finish this grant proposal. Don't worry, it'll happen.*

Every time I looked at my aunt and uncle, I had to clench my right hand harder against my stinging eyes and the pain in the back of my throat. Tears were a luxury to be enjoyed by other people. Once, by accident, I squeezed both hands and Leslie flinched and withdrew hers, giving me a glance and rubbing her fingers.

Afterwards, Law's older sister, Susan, sobbed into Dylan's lapel. I tried to say something to Aunt Sharon, but when I got down to it, there didn't seem to be any words that fit. All the obvious consolations had no doubt been used up by then, and all that was left was the truth – that their lives would go on without him – a bargain no parent makes when bringing a child into the world...

The *padre* looked like he was preparing to say the homily now. He still had a shock of black hair, but the lines on his forehead and around his eyes said he'd borne his orders a long time. He read out the text from the Gospel of John. I picked out words like *luz* and *mundo*, *oscuridad* and *no lo ha entendido*. A light that no one understood. So people chose darkness instead.

I smelled the darkness of fresh, wet earth on a barely man-sized coffin, the family standing around, outlined by late-falling sunlight, and knew that I did not understand.

For some reason, I thought of a line from a poem by Dylan Thomas that Leslie had scrawled across one of her notebooks: "Time held me green and dying / though I sang in my chains like the sea."

We stood to sing the final hymn.

I squinted into the bright sunlight outside of the church. I felt like I was seeing in negative. Shouldn't the church be full of light, the darkness hovering just beyond?

It had been the most brilliant of sunny mornings when Dad had died, too... I shook my head and looked around for Dylan and Rachel.

Several women were grouped together, speaking softly, while the men set up a few folding tables and carried out a couple of the more battered pews that doubled as picnic benches. The smell of smoke, *mole*, and fresh tortillas drifted out from the kitchen, a lean-to of scrap wood and sheet metal built onto the back of the church.

I stood away from the side door as men came out of the church with a final bench. Dylan stepped up and took a hold, although they seemed to be handling it well enough without him. Raquel was carrying steaming pots of food out from the back. I shifted from foot to foot, wondering whether they would understand me if I offered to help. My conversational Spanish was still minimal and definitely didn't extend to church events.

As I looked around, a man in faded blue plaid smiled and beckoned me over to where he was seated at one of the picnic tables. Well, it wouldn't take long for him to realize I didn't speak Spanish, but here was a distraction at least. A moment later, I felt a stab of guilt for that thought. His left leg ended in a wooden stump. I sat down beside him.

"*Buenas dias. ¿Hables Español?*"

I balked. I knew this. Why was I thinking of Latin verbs from my years at a classical high school?

"*¿No hables Español?*" He looked me over. "*¿Americano?*"

"Yes – *sí.*"

"*Yo entiendo un poquito de Ingles, pero no hablo Inglés bien.*" He raised his voice and spoke slowly, taking care with each word. "*¿Cómo te llamas? Me llamo Juan.*"

"Oh, *sí* – I mean..." I wasn't sure how much he meant by *un poquito de Inglés*, or if I would be able to decipher his responses in Spanish, but it seemed rude not to reciprocate. "*Me llamo* Jim."

He nodded, his smile revealing stained teeth.

What could I ask that he might understand? I couldn't remember the Spanish word for work. "Do you have a job?"

The man smiled but shook his head. I tried again, enunciating more clearly.

"Do you work?"

"*Oh, sí. Soy pescador.*"

I exhaled. "A fisherman."

The man bobbed his head.

"What fish do you catch? *¿Que pescado?*"

The man grinned wider. "*Cabrillo... mucho cabrillo.*"

I nodded. What now? I lacked the vocabulary to ask him how it was to be a one-legged fisherman.

"The service was good." I bit my tongue. I hadn't paid enough attention to the priest, really.

"*¿Que?*"

"The church service – " I fumbled through my memory for a Spanish approximation. None came.

"*Ah, la iglesia –* "

"*Sí* – yes..." I looked at the church building as if it could help me with conversational Spanish.

"*Es bonita. ¿No?*"

"*Sí.*"

"*Ayudé en la construcción.*"

I blinked. The man nodded, his eyes on the whitewashed church.

Raquel walked over, touching my arm as she sat down: "Need a translator?"

"You have *no* idea."

She said something to the man too quickly for me to attempt to distinguish the words. He answered.

"He says he – he thought maybe you were lonely, standing there by yourself."

The directness of her gaze stripped me bare. I wondered if I was already consigned to the category of pitiable.

I thought for a second. "If he's a fisherman, can you ask if he knows any good spot south of here to go spearfishing?"

By the time Raquel had translated another exchange or two – good diving at the next bay south, so Juan had heard – the *padre* called everyone to prayer, and the feasting began.

The rich, chocolaty spice of chicken *mole*, refried pinto beans, *salsa fresca* – every flavor had such incredible vitality – as if until now I'd been tasting in black and white.

"Glad you came to church with me instead of going to the *cantina*?" Raquel surveyed us from across the table.

"Hell – ah – heck yeah!" Dylan said.

"What do they do in that kitchen – dark arts?" My upper lip was sweaty from the peppers, but I couldn't stop eating.

Raquel laughed. "Every self-respecting Mexican woman can cook like this. My grandmother taught me how to when I was a kid."

"I grew up in California. Which used to be Mexico. So where has this been all my life?" Dylan's eyes locked on hers, although he gestured to the chicken on his fork.

"It's just that most Americans feel the need to Americanize everything they encounter, and that usually means a lot less flavor. The inevitable homogenization of everything smacking of *sabor*," Raquel shrugged. "It's sad, but I don't think it's about to change."

"So, how about it?" Dylan said, looking at us both.

Neither of us knew what we were meant to be thinking.

"Sailing – Raquel joining us – augmenting our crew by one – possibly getting her to cook occasionally in exchange for us paying for all the food and kneeling at her feet and thanking her for her beneficence."

"Hmm." Raquel looked at both of us.

We waited.

"Let me see the boat, first of all."

"Hell yeah! I knew you'd do it!"

Raquel smiled. "I haven't said yes, yet, Dylan. I'm staying at my cousin's here, so I'll probably have her husband come and grill you both before I commit to anything. And that's if you're lucky and I like the boat."

Dylan beamed at her. After a moment's gloating, he went to get more *mole*.

I looked over at Raquel. I'd had a question in mind to ask her just two seconds ago. But when our eyes met, my throat tightened and my tongue stayed resolutely still. I listened in dismay to the ever-expanding silence.

Raquel, however, seemed unselfconscious as ever. "So I think you missed the part where we discussed what a good sailor I am." She winked.

I blinked. "I – ah – trust Dylan's judgment." Well that was a stretch, but admitting that I hadn't thought of her qualifications till this moment seemed too unseamanlike a slip to acknowledge.

We sat there a moment, quiet again, with laughter and conversation and feasting all around us.

Finally, I had a question: "So what brings you here?"

Dammit! She'd already said she was visiting a cousin.

"I'm taking a year off to travel. Thought I'd start by visiting family, you know?"

I nodded. How old was she? Taking a year off from what? Dylan appeared engrossed in a culinary discussion with one of the women who had cooked the meal. Somehow he was picking Spanish up again much more rapidly than I. This confirmed my theory that some people are naturally good at languages – Dylan being one of them, myself, not.

I turned back to Raquel, willing myself to say *something*. "And where else do you want to go?"

She took a deep breath: "Peru, Chile, Argentina. Spain, France, Italy. Turkey, Morocco, South Africa. Nepal, India, Cambodia. Australia. For starters." She laughed at me – I guess my jaw was gaping. "I'm sure I won't make it everywhere this time. I just want to put a dent in the list."

I exhaled, nodding. I'd known another woman who loved to travel. I shook my head.

"What? You don't think I can handle it?"

"I – no, absolutely – I was... thinking of something else."

"Oh," she shoved her beans around with her fork.

"I'm interested in what you're saying, honest, I just – " I gave myself a mental kick in the shins, "you reminded me of someone else for a second."

"Someone nice, I hope." She smiled.

I tried to smile back.

Two days later, after the boat inspection, an evening meal at Raquel's cousin Rosaria's house, and a day trip down to the bay Rosaria's husband confirmed was full of fish (so Raquel could demonstrate her experience and we could spear a few fish), I made an entry in the logbook beyond my usual recording of latitude, longitude, and miles sailed:

Today we took on a third crew member. Her name is Raquel Peña, and she has agreed to sail with us as our chef, first mate, and translator. In return, we (as co-captains) have undertaken to cover all expenses, provide all food and entertainment (e.g., cerveza), and drop her at whatever port she desires along our route. All hands in high spirits at this new addition and a fair wind blowing, which we take as a favorable omen – all superstitions regarding women on sailing vessels notwithstanding.

I looked up from the logbook as voices sounded on deck. Raquel must be bringing her luggage aboard. A moment later, footsteps tattooed on the companionway and Raquel and Dylan both appeared at the other end of the cabin that served as galley, living space and office. Dylan was lugging a large rucksack and a cardboard box.

"We stopped at the *supermercado* for some last-minute shopping." Dylan nodded. "Our cooking supplies were weighed in the balance and found wanting."

I put down my pen and came over to glance in the box. "I didn't know cayenne peppers were one of those food items you should always have on hand."

Raquel nodded: "Which is why I am the cook and you are not."

"Thank God!" Dylan said, a little too fervently.

I turned to Raquel: "Would you like to see your quarters, now that they're less cluttered?"

"Of course!"

"It's small," I said.

"We spent hours throwing junk out last night," Dylan added. I frowned at him.

"You shouldn't have gone to so much trouble."

"We're looking for excuses to be chivalrous," said Dylan. "But please let me set this down somewhere, before I have to beg."

"Everything ship-shape?" Raquel appeared from below, her oversized white sun shirt fluttering in the breeze, her long brown legs finding an easy stance on the deck.

I nodded: "Aye-aye, sailor." Great. The return of Awkward Jim. I looked up at the swelling sails. "We're making good time with this wind. Maybe five or six knots."

I'd taken extra care with the calculations and had been waiting a while to share this knowledge.

I felt my eyes swing back to her like a compass to magnetic north. She was looking up at the mizzenmast now, a hand on her Padres cap to make sure it stayed. Yet another reason to like her. Watching her, I thought that maybe I caught a glimpse of the truth behind things. I couldn't look away, although she'd catch me soon.

"Whaddup?"

Dylan returned from the bow of the boat, where he'd been obeying the call of nature. We hadn't quite gotten used to the fact that we now had a third crew member who might not appreciate this practice, no matter how much more efficient peeing over the side of the boat was. Dylan's eyes flicked between Raquel, who was standing near the wheel, and me. I had become deeply engrossed in my role as pilot.

"Not much." I followed Dylan's practice and kept my gaze on the horizon.

"I'm just basking in the feeling of *really* sailing," Raquel said, smiling serenely.

Dylan smiled at her in a way I was sure her cousin would disapprove of: I certainly did. It was ...possessive.

"Want me to take the helm, Jimbo?"

I gritted my teeth. Dylan *knew* I hated that nickname. Now Raquel might think it meant something about who I was. Uncle Ernie called me that the first time Dad had taken us down to Baja. I had finally worked up the courage to tell my uncle I disliked the nickname, and Uncle Ernie had said I could choose my own name once I could swim out to the rock and back. It had taken me two years to earn the right of being "Just Jim," and on that technicality, Uncle Ernie had still won, in a sense.

Leslie had started out calling me James, flirted briefly with Jim, and ended with Jimmy, which seemed like a very Benjamin Button-esque progression for a name.

While caught up in this pointless mental soliloquy, I yielded the wheel to Dylan, who had Raquel standing in front of him at the helm in ten seconds flat. Apparently she'd never steered anything bigger than a *panga*. I went forward, found myself a patch of sunshine between the zodiac and other paraphernalia, and went to sleep.

I woke to the smell of jasmine. For a second, eyes still closed, I thought I was at my grandparents' house again, with the scents of flowering vines and sunshine drifting in through the French doors.

"Jim."

That wasn't Gran's voice, though it warmed me still, as did the hand resting on my shoulder. I wrenched my eyes open. The taste of sleep mingled with the over-exposed feeling of too much sunlight. Raquel knelt beside me, her eyes unsearchable in the brightness behind her.

"Want some lunch? I made seafood omelets."

I nodded, blinking.

We slipped over the side of the anchored boat and into the water. Raquel trod water as she adjusted her mouthpiece. Then, with a thumbs-up to me and Dylan, she started off. It was strange to be following a girl on a snorkeling expedition, but maybe that just showed my limited experience. Actually, I was used to leading the way myself – whether I *knew* the way or not. But Raquel knew these waters from longer excursions she'd taken with her family, and she was an experienced diver in her own right.

We swam in a line: Raquel, myself, Dylan. I watched her fins beat the water up ahead. Her long braid danced like an eel behind her as her head turned back and forth, searching for markers for the secret spot she'd told us about. The water was so warm I imagined the sun's early rays piercing the surface to caress my back. This part of the little bay was still and clear, sheltered by a headland that also hid it from the eyes of unenlightened sailors.

Out of the corner of my eye, I caught a movement in the seaweed. Fish, seal, or...? My heart rate doubled for a second. Then I dragged my imagination away from the Jules Vernean monsters that had peopled the oceans of my childhood. I could hear nothing save my own raspy breathing through the snorkel and the muted rhythm of swells against the cliff-like part of the shore. We swam along till we came to the large rock that "stood solitary out from the headland". Here Raquel turned her masked eyes back toward us to make sure we were still following, and then dove down.

The water cooled as we angled steeply for the bottom. A flurry of anchovies flashed away to my left. As I got a better look at the wall of bone-colored rock to my right, it came to life. Cranberry and orange starfish clung to the rock, some with as many as nine arms. Beside them, sea anemones bloomed among barnacles and amber seaweed.

My thirst for oxygen forced me up. When I returned from the surface, Raquel and Dylan were on the ocean floor. I gave a couple of good scissor kicks and joined them. Raquel was pointing at little bubbles rising up from the golden sand. She started digging fast, following the bubbles, and soon held up a big *chocolata* clam. I loosened the mouth of my ditty bag and began to dig. Though I nearly exhausted my breath, I came up with nothing but sand. Raquel pointed to the surface. Dylan and I followed her up.

She took out her mouthpiece: "You have to dig faster than the clams. They start burrowing as soon as you start digging toward them."

Dylan and I nodded, treading water in silence like we were back in swim class.

"I'll point out a couple of spots for lobster while we're at it, but this is one of the best spots for *chocolatas*, so ..."

We plunged back into the pale green water, pixilated by the strengthening sun.

Dylan and I soon grasped the basics of diving for clams – a thing Dad had never taught us. I wondered why. He and Uncle Ernie had spent so much of the last forty years in Baja, they must have picked up just about every skill known to man – at least where the ocean was concerned. Most of that knowledge (or the rudiments thereof) he'd passed on to us.

When our ditty bags grew heavy, we tied them, submerged, to the back of the boat to keep the clams fresh. Then we swam to the strip of beach along the little cove and fell back in the sand. Or, eyes shielded from the glint of the sun off the water, sat and watched pelicans diving out past the curve of brown bluff to the north.

The aroma of hot sand and saltwater drying on skin smelled like home. And then there was the heat, combined with that distinct tiredness that comes with any kind of exertion in water. I closed my eyes.

When I woke, my tongue felt thick, and I thought for a second I was back in my own bed. Then I heard a snort and opened my eyes.

Raquel was leaning over me, her hair now free from its braid and sandy at the tips. For a millisecond my stomach did not wholly unpleasant backflips. Then I saw what was in her right hand, just inches from my chest. She held a mottled shell between index finger and thumb. Little red legs poked out from the bottom. A hermit crab. By the time I realized what it was, Raquel had set it on my sternum. I felt a dribble of seawater and the tickle of the escaping crab. Only, he was making his escape the wrong way; up toward my neck.

Oh *hell* no. I shouted and sat up, grabbing for it blindly.

"Jim! Oh no! Now where has he gone? Hermes!" She dove into the sand behind me in search of it.

I stared daggers at Raquel.

"Thank goodness! Look, you scared him." Eyes wide and guileless, she turned her palm toward me, where the red legs had almost entirely disappeared under the shell.

"*Pobrecito*," she cooed.

"Dammit, Raquel – !"

Her eyes held something akin to a twinkle, and I heard a second snort from my other side. I rolled over and sucker-punched Dylan.

Raquel jumped up and ran to the water's edge. I thought she was making her escape before the sand really began to fly, but then she came back, sans Hermes.

"Help!" I gasped, because Raquel had distracted me long enough for Dylan to mount his counterattack.

She grinned and fell to her knees, running her fingers lightly along Dylan's rib cage.

"Hey! No tickling! That's fighting dirty!" Dylan gave up trying to pummel me and grabbed both her wrists.

I was prepared to count this a victory, until I caught sight of her face. Raquel was laughing and gasping for help in her turn, but her cheeks were flushed and her eyes luminous. I felt a squirm of that green serpent, jealousy.

IV.

"Who wants another drink?"

My hand raced up, along with two others.

I turned to Dylan: "Did you just raise your hand in to answer to your own question?"

"Shut up or you don't get one."

I closed my mouth promptly. Dylan disappeared toward the galley, switching on the small companionway light as he went down.

Raquel was humming the chorus of a song she couldn't remember the name of or what band it was by. She'd appealed to Dylan and me earlier, and we had been wildly unhelpful. I had suggested Pink Floyd or Aerosmith; Dylan had said Vampire Weekend or Band of Horses. She'd shaken her head at us and kept humming: "I know I'll figure it out eventually." Meanwhile, it was stuck in all our heads.

Now, she stood up and shook out the Aztec blanket she'd had across her lap. She spread it over the still-warm wood of the deck and lay down, her head tilted to the myriad stars of a Baja night sky. After a moment, she raised her head and looked at me.

"Come look." She patted a spot on the blanket.

My hands locked to my camp chair. I sat there for a moment, an unnamed fear threatening to engulf me. Then I released my fingers one at a time, walked over and lowered myself onto the blanket beside her. I was all at once very conscious of my arms. Suppose I laid my left arm beside me, and my hand bumped against her thigh. She might think I was the kind of guy to exploit a budding friendship and close quarters. I could, alternatively, reach my arm around her shoulders as a more forthright expression of affection (friendly or otherwise). Or I could – suiting the action to the thought – fold my arms behind my head and avoid all swampy questions of feeling, for the time being.

I glanced at her without turning my head. She was staring up, wide-eyed, at the stars, her face relaxing under their lidless gaze. She kept her eyes heavenward as she said:

"Do you know any of the myths about the stars? My *abuelo* used to tell me stories. I'm pretty sure he improvised whenever he felt like the originals weren't good enough."

I shook my head against the wool of the blanket. "My – my dad and my uncle would point out constellations, but I don't think they knew the stories behind them. They were more interested in using the stars for navigation."

"Tell me about them. Your dad and uncle."

Just at that moment, Dylan emerged from below decks. I heard him on the stairs and exhaled slowly. He held three margaritas on a tray, and his eyes glowed strangely in the light coming from below.

"Raquel was asking me about Dad and Uncle Ernie," I said, thinking I should probably get off the blanket, or at least edge a little further away from Raquel.

"Oh yeah?"

"Before that, we were talking about constellations." I nodded superfluously at the sky. "Sounds like you have some good stories," I said in Raquel's general direction.

"Yeah, Raquel," said Dylan, setting down the drinks and settling himself on her other side, despite the fact that there was less blanket there. "Let's hear more about the stars."

I could only see her in profile, but I guessed by the sudden, chiseled stillness of Raquel's features that she had picked up on the veiled hostility in Dylan's voice, though perhaps she'd mistaken its target. I wanted to reassure her that this really had nothing to do with her – that this brotherly enmity was as old as Adam's sons – but I couldn't quite convince myself that this was the case.

"Okay," Raquel said coolly, "where should I start?"

She lay quiet so long I wondered whether she'd fallen asleep, or decided to tap out after all. But then she spoke:

"Once upon a time, there were two boys, and the boys were best friends. When they were still very young, their fathers began to train them in the ways of the forest. As they grew, they learned to be hunting partners – how to track a bird, a rabbit, even a deer – how to signal one another if there was game nearby – and how to defend each other from the attacks of wolves or mountain lions. In the course of time, they both brought meat back to their mothers' hearth fires. After that, they were allowed to sit with the men. Late at night, they sat around the hunting fires and listened to the old men tell stories. There it was they first heard whispers of a Sacred Bear of the Mountain, who could kill or bless a man with a single glance.

"One day when the boys were fourteen or fifteen, they went hunting further up in the mountains than usual. For a long time now, their village had suffered from a drought – their crops would not grow and their wells were dry or putrid – even the wild animals had deserted their land for more fertile country.

"Today, with no kills and the day far spent, Victor – the older one – went into a dark stand of trees to look for game, while Marcus patrolled outside to make sure they were not ambushed by the still-prowling wolves.

"Victor pressed through undergrowth so dense it seemed to form a kind of wall against him, the more so as he came to the heart of the thicket. The sun was waning, but as he pushed at last into the opening at the center of the woods, it looked as though twilight already had fallen.

"His eye caught a movement ahead and he drew an arrow from his quiver. Then he stood transfixed, unable even to replace the arrow. Before him, her face partly obscured from view by a cascade of dark hair, was a girl. A fawn rested its muzzle in her lap, and her hand caressed it as if it were a pup. Her bare shoulders rose free and graceful above her peasant's dress.

"The boy watched her in silence, as he had been trained to watch prey before striking. Only, this time, he felt himself at *her* mercy.

"He could tell that she knew he was there, but she did not look up at him. He wanted to call to her, to throw himself at her feet and, if he dared, gaze into her eyes, but he could not move. Even when he heard his friend whistling their signal and then calling out – Marcus, his friend from his youth and his hunting companion – he could not bear to answer him. What if he frightened her away and never saw her again and never for one instant gazed upon the secret locked within her eyes?

"Finally, after an eternity of waiting, she raised her head from the fawn and turned and looked Victor full in the face.

"All this time, Marcus was growing more and more anxious as he waited for his friend outside the thicket. He thought of all the fates that could have befallen Victor: eaten by a cougar, torn by wolves, ensnared in one of the traps inferior hunters sometimes used to catch game – a cruel way, especially if they did not check their traps often and the animal had to die slowly, with all the blood pooled in its head. He didn't dare think of the Bear.

"At last, after whistling their signal several times to no avail, and no longer able to bear the vast silence, Marcus called out Victor's name. No answer. He paced to and fro. Again, he called the name familiar to him as his own. No answer. He decided he must go after Victor, even if that meant risking whatever fate had befallen his friend.

"At first, it grew darker and darker as he pushed through the tightly growing trees and grasping vines. They seemed to go on far longer than they should have, given the size of the thicket. Then there was a flash of illumination, followed by a moonlit glow that came from the heart of the undergrowth. Marcus pushed forward, his heart pounding, no longer attempting to guess what he would find.

"What he saw held him for a second motionless. A luminous being clutched Victor to her, her mouth clamped against his own. Such was Marcus's innocence, and such the practices of their small village, that he had never before seen a man and a woman in a passionate embrace, and he imagined her to be a demon, sucking the life from his friend.

"Without hesitation, but taking careful aim, he strung an arrow and let fly.

"At the same moment, Victor caught sight of Marcus and the arrow and, crying out, flung himself in front of it. He caught the arrow in the heart and was dead before Marcus could drop his bow and run to his friend's side.

"Marcus clutched Victor close and looked up, groaning, into the face of the one he had taken for his friend's killer. He knew his mistake as soon as their eyes met.

"'Help me!' he cried. 'Let me join him – since it is too late to bring him back.'

"'That is your desire?' she said, her eyes showering tears over Victor's frame, moonglow slowly ebbing from her face.

"'I have killed my friend, who was more to me than a brother. I now wish for nothing in the world but to leave it and be with him once more.'

"'Very well.' She took a thin blade from the bosom of her dress and handed it to Marcus. He drew a long breath, looked at her and then at Victor once more, and drove it deep into his chest. Blood burst forth and flowed freely on his friend's feet as he fell.

"The girl watched them there a long while. Then, she waved her hands slowly over each of them. When she turned her palms upward, she held two handfuls of what looked like diamonds. Rising to her full height, which was far greater than one would have believed, she emerged from the wood and walked through the thickening dusk, till she came to the precipice of a mountain. Standing there and murmuring to herself, she cast the glittering stones up into the sky. There they stayed, taking the shapes of two bears, shining over a valley that would no more be plagued by drought. Turning, the girl's shape changed and she too was a great bear, roaring out her age-old sadness across the sleeping valley."

There was a moment of harmonic silence.

"And that's my *abuelo's* origin story for *Ursa Major* and *Ursa Minor*."

We all lay still for a long spell, looking upward. The lights of the Little and Big Dippers – easier to trace than their parent constellations, the Bears – burned like torches, and stars I was sure I'd never seen before shone in between the brighter ones. Together, they formed the luminous profile of an otherworldly city.

For a single, sacred moment, I wanted things to be no different from precisely how they were. Then Raquel shivered and I moved to put my arm around her shoulder. But my arm brushed another, smoother than my own but still a man's, reaching from her other side. I recoiled.

Raquel cleared her throat, and Dylan – arm still in place – said, "That's like no Greek myth I've heard before."

"My grandfather probably combined a few stories he'd heard at various points. Anyway, the point of oral storytelling isn't accuracy – it's the quality of the story ..."

They continued to rib each other, but I stopped listening, got up, and walked to the prow of the boat, saying I needed "some air."

The night was still, and just balmy enough to feel like a shy caress, instead of a hand pressing down on you. I thought about Dad showing Dylan and me how to find the North Star starting from the Big Dipper. He'd held Dylan on his hip, even though Dylan was far too big by that point. We stood in the tomato patch in the back yard one evening with no moon, looking up. I could almost smell the tomatoes now, watching the twinkling sky and wondering how it was possible so vividly to conjure up memories, yet have no communion with the ghosts who lived there.

When I came back, I found Dylan and Raquel back in their respective chairs, drinking margaritas and talking about great white sharks. Dylan handed me a drink, ever-so-slightly unsteady. I took a sip. By now the ice had melted, but even that couldn't mellow the kick from the tequila.

Dylan must have been eyeballing the shots again when he mixed the drinks. Maybe he wasn't cut out for bartending.

I resumed my seat.

A coyote's howl drifted out from shore on the night air. Raquel shivered. I could feel the hairs at the nape of my neck rise. A few yips told us that other coyotes prowled in the scrub not far from the beach. They pulled me back to the Baja of my childhood. Hearing coyotes as you lay on your cot on the beach and almost – but not quite – believing Uncle Ernie when he said they'd eat you if the dogs didn't sleep by your side all night. So you lay awake a while and talked to your brother and made sure the dogs stayed close by and watched the Big and Little Dippers as they stared back at you in the clear black night.

Dylan picked up the conversation where I'd interrupted: "I think the great white I was closest to was in Lompoc. Jim was in college by then, but I was fresh out of high school."

I glanced over. I'd never heard this story before.

"One of my friends got a sweet VW bus for his birthday – pimped out with a stove and a sink and curtains – and he wanted to take a road trip with it as soon as school was out. It must have been early June, and the sun never stopped shining as we drove down the 101. We took that kind of luck for granted back then. We spent a night in Refugio, then headed straight for San Diego to do whatever seventeen and eighteen-year-olds do there."

"And what is that?" said Raquel.

"Um ...Use fake IDs to buy booze, surf, pretend you like smoking joints, hit on all the pretty girls on the beaches, eat – a lot..." He chuckled.

I said: "Well, that's what *you* were doing at eighteen. The summer after my senior year, I had to take an extra class to prep for my freshman calculus course and refold clothes at Gap, because not all of us can ace tests without studying and have college football scholarships fall into our laps."

As soon as the words were out, I wanted to hit rewind and erase them. I sounded like a disgruntled kid accusing the other baseball team of cheating, just because they'd won.

There was a pause.

I coughed. "So, when did you see the shark?"

"Yeah. Well, we were going to drive straight back after four days of surfing and chilling in San Diego, but my buddy Evan got tired, and he wouldn't let any of us drive his baby, so we pulled off Highway 1 around Lompoc and slept by the road. The next morning was golden. The cars woke us up early: locals on their way to the ocean, boards strapped to roofs or poking out of windows or truck beds.

"The surf had to be great. So we ate cold pepperoni pizza from the night before and Evan drove. Sure enough, Surf Beach was breaking clean four to five footers. The water was turquoise and spotted with surfers riding or waiting for the next wave.

"Evan pulled into the parking lot like a Formula 1 driver while the rest of us were wrestling on wetsuits, still damp from our last surf session at Black's. Then we all grabbed our boards and raced for the water. The waves were as great as they'd looked from shore; it clouded over a little, but other than that it was the perfect surf sesh. We were all getting barreled and making the locals show some respect.

"We'd probably been in the water an hour before I saw the fin. If you're a surfer," I could tell from the quality of Dylan's voice that his head was turned toward Raquel, "you know you can't afford to suspect every bird, seal, dolphin, or even shark of being a great white. So I told myself it was fine. I kept paddling for a few seconds, but something made me look again. It really was a fin, and it wasn't a dolphin's fin, or any other fin I'd ever seen in the ocean before. It was mouse-colored and huge and it cut in from the open water a little too fast.

"I hesitated for a second. I would look like a complete dumbass if it turned out to be anything less deadly than a great white. Of course, as happens in these situations, nobody was close enough to give a second opinion."

"You actually thought about saying nothing?" Raquel's voice was sharp.

"Yeah, I did. I was eighteen and, I guess, still coming to terms with realities like death. I looked again and it was about fifteen yards away. I caught a glimpse of a white snout and I knew. Not because I could have identified it from my marine biology textbook. I just knew – in my gut. At the same time, I finally realized what the upshot would be if I didn't get everyone out: blood flushing from loose limbs and the screams of my friends and the locals. It took a second to make any sound come out of my mouth. Then I started yelling.

"Well, these Lompoc surfers are used to evacuations, and they cleared the water *fast*. And, no joke, I paddled ashore quicker than I ever have in my life. I realized afterwards that I'd heard about this place in connection with great whites before. It was also on a sign we passed, walking back to the VW: "Warning: Fatal Shark Attacks. Swim/Surf at Your Own Risk." It was in Spanish too, and somebody had written in sloppy cursive: "*Veridad*, Shark." It was true. An older surfer saw the fin too and told me I'd saved a lot of lives. I think he also gave me a swig of something strong, because my legs were about to fold under me."

"¡*Madre de Dios*!" said Raquel.

"Wait!" Dylan said.

She sucked in her breath.

"I forgot to tell you the best part of the story. So, I was yelling "Shark!" and watching everyone paddle like they were trying to catch the wave of the year, and it took a few seconds for me to remember that *I* hadn't moved yet.

"I looked behind me and the shark seemed to be coming faster than ever. I paddled – *hard*. I was one of the last people in the water, and I remember looking back once and seeing him – or her, I won't be sexist about it – coming like death and taxes."

"Meaning –?" I said.

"Meaning, unavoidably. But a wave was forming – "

I snorted. It sounded like a script for one of those numerous, B-rated surfer movies.

"Dammit, Jim! It's a true story, so help me. The only reason I caught the wave was because I had to. My body knew it was time to perform and it did. I surfed in and didn't stop until my fin was stuck in the sand – after which I heroically puked and we all saw the yellow "*¡Precautión!*" sign. I still see "*Tiberon fatal*" in black letters sometimes in nightmares."

"Oh, Dylan." That was Raquel.

"So why didn't you tell me – or anyone?" I tried to keep my voice neutral, balanced.

"Oh, I did tell – a few people."

Just not your brother.

"Just talk to Evan if you don't believe me. Or read the Fish and Wildlife report."

"But Dad never said anything – "

"I didn't tell him." Dylan paused. "It's weird to try to tell the people you – to tell your family – that you almost died. After the fact. Being eighteen didn't make it easier, either. And remember I was only home for the summer – I'd been living with Mom, and... I wasn't gonna tell her. Dad wasn't home when I got back, and by the time he got home I'd decided he was happier not knowing, since I wasn't gonna change the way I was living my life, anyway."

"Dylan! I can't believe you almost died and never talked to your own parents about it," said Raquel. "But how about your friends? They never told, either?"

"I fed them some bullshit about Dad saying we needed time to heal and that no one was supposed to talk about the incident. As if Dad would say anything remotely like that. But whether I convinced them or not, Evan and the gang never brought it up unless we were alone."

I wanted to see Dylan's expression, but he was on the further side of Raquel, sheltered from a brother's prying eyes. Anyway, it was pretty dark.

I slouched down in my chair. This silence was different, if only to me. I was starting to realize the weight of the things Dylan and I had kept from each other.

Our boys' years' secrets had always been shared. Like the fact that Columbus Day was not actually a school holiday – in our school district, at least. After Mom left, we'd managed to convince Dad that schools closed in honor of the so-called Discoverer of the Americas. Of course, any time we felt like a break, we had another method of conning him. Dad would wave us off from the window as we walked to the bus stop. As soon as we turned the corner, we'd circle back around the block and climb up into our tree fort, which we'd smuggled provisions out to the night before. Dylan would doctor Dad's signatures on our excused absence forms, while I scanned the neighborhood with binoculars, checking whether any of our friends had convinced their moms that their stomachaches or sore throats were genuine.

The year I was twelve or thirteen had been one of the best. That was before my conscience had begun to smart noticeably at this traditional deception, and also before I'd started going to high school, where excused absences were more complicated. We were already getting too old for the fort, but we excused it on grounds of practicality. When I scanned the perimeter one bright morning in early November, I spotted boys in two yards, furiously waving bandanas – the signal of success.

We met at the appointed place – near a stand of eucalyptus at the base of Bishop's Peak, one of the extinct volcanoes that brooded over our lives.

I carried a pack of supplies: water, beef jerky, red vines, root beer – all the Friday night snacks we'd been able to convince Dad to buy and restrain ourselves from eating. I also had a tarp, "in case it rains." Dylan brought matches – in case we got stuck somewhere and had to build a fire. These, "Strike Anywhere," he'd smuggled one by one from the box above the mantle. The caution of taking one at a time was probably wasted on Dad, but it made it feel more like an undercover operation. Dylan also had a deck of cards, *The Best of Calvin and Hobbes* (or a title to similar effect), and a book for identifying the wild animals of California.

Our fellow delinquents – Evan and Jason – brought Cheetos and fruit leather, respectively. Jason's parents were Health Nuts, Dad said.

I also carried a staff, like one of the fifteen companions from *The Hobbit*. Dylan wore a hat that could do everything: carry water to put out your campfire, fly through the air and strike your enemies, or impress the girls in your neighborhood. So far, Dylan had had most success with the last function. He'd already kissed a couple, while I, on the other hand, had yet to hold a girl's hand.

We set off on the hike. I told them what we should do if we – hypothetically – met any wild animals. Dylan pulled his slingshot from his back pocket and casually picked up a couple of small rocks when I mentioned mountain lions. We knew – well, mostly knew – that we were far more likely to see vultures and rabbits, but reminding ourselves of all possible eventualities added a little excitement. This was the first time we'd set out to climb to the top of Bishop's without Dad. In previous years, we'd been satisfied playing Battleship or Risk in the tree fort and making the occasional foray around the back of our neighborhood, where it embraced the swelling roots of the mountain.

The day was one of those gold and blue ones of Indian Summer – warm, but with the taste of fall – fermenting apples, fresh-turned earth and wood smoke – in the breeze. As we sweated up the first steep ascent, rutted from old rains and cracked for lack of new ones, a roadrunner skittered across our path. Evan, whose parents were not Health Nuts and who had recently moved here from the Valley, squeaked between labored breaths.

"What's that?" He stared into the brush. He'd only caught the sound – the bird itself wouldn't frighten anyone.

Dylan and I exchanged glances. Evan was a *gringo*. We would have to teach him that very few animals deserved his fear. Jason knew. He had been successfully getting additional days off with us for the past three years. His parents had practically raised him among wolf pups – they would have, but all they had on hand were a few chickens and a rescue dog. Still, he'd known the difference between red-tailed and kestrel hawks at age five, and had spotted and caught those shy horny toads almost from the time he could walk. But his parents didn't teach him anything about weaponry, so it was up to the brothers West to defend our band if we encountered a mountain lion or a rabid coyote or a black bear.

Or a man. Dad had warned us about a certain type of man who would offer us candy or a ride in his car or something else as a kind of fishing lure. Then, when he got us where he wanted us, well. Dad had looked like he'd rather be puking at this point in the conversation, but instead he gave us a rough sketch of what might happen. We got this talk well before "the talk," which seemed redundant at the point Dad broached it. Our sex ed classes in school had long since come and gone, leaving us caught between curiosity and disbelief that these things were really so. As we got older, it seemed less and less strange.

For now, though, hiking for a welcome shady moment among live oaks, all that mattered was our trek to the peak.

"Do you have your compass?" Dylan said.

I fished around in my camo shirt pocket. How had I forgotten to use it when we started out? I pulled out the compass and tried to keep my hand perfectly steady. It was harder to read than you thought.

"Well?" Dylan said, after a near silence – Evan was still breathing heavily in the background.

"North-west," I said, making my voice as authoritative as possible. "What time is it?" I looked at Dylan, who looked at his watch, which had slid to the underside of his wrist.

"Ten hundred hours." Dylan always said it just like an army commander from *The Great Escape* or something. I pulled out a golf pencil and a piece of printer paper I'd borrowed from Dad's office and noted down both items.

"Shouldn't we have a snack now?" Evan said.

"No, we need to save our provisions for when the going gets tough," I said, like Dad always did, although I badly wanted some Cheetos and CapriSun right now.

"But – "

"You heard him," Dylan said.

We were a united front, like the Allies in World War II. Well, like the good allies, not like Russia, which hadn't been much different from Germany, in the end.

We trudged on up the mountain, our feet kicking up a haze of milky-white dust. The sun shone full on us now, and I could feel my toes slipping against each other, growing grittier with each step from the dirt that filtered into my socks through my sneakers.

The smell of hot dirt combined with the wild sweetness of sagebrush and chaparral. Evan whimpered, and I took pity on him and called a halt. We drank water from the general canteen, because – for once – water sounded better than soda, and ate Cheetos till the orange stickiness on our fingers seemed impervious to licks. I took a moment to survey the view, pointing out to Evan how far we'd already come and how small the cows looked where they picked over distant brown fields for food.

Shouldering our packs again, the West party turned once more toward the mountainside. Hands and legs were required for this next section (my favorite), where you climbed between two rocks the size of elephants' backs, and then the path got so steep that if you didn't hang on by your fingernails to rocks or branches you might slip.

We were all huffing a little by now. Dylan led the way. Shimmying quickly up a large boulder in the trail, his foot skidded on loose gravel near the top and he fell, hitting against an outcropping of the rock on the way down.

I ran over to him.

Dylan lay, clutching his knee, his head turned sideways away from us and his eyes blinking hard.

"Shit!"

"Dylan!" I couldn't think what else to say. "Dylan Michael West!"

"What?" His voice was swollen and mutinous.

"You know we aren't supposed to cuss."

Evan shifted uneasily, and Jason snickered. I saw that I held onto my position as leader by a fraying thread. I looked at Dylan. I wasn't sure how to tell if someone had injured his head, but I thought if he could swear, he was probably okay.

Dylan sat up but kept his eyes lowered, running a finger over the scrape. "Fine, then. Damn." He looked up at me, a challenge in his eyes, as I knelt to look at his knee. The boys, standing back a little along the trail, snorted.

I breathed in carefully, trying to remember how Dad handled wounds. I also tried not to feel robbed that Dylan had gotten to use those words before me.

I pulled out the canteen. "We need to wash the junk off so it doesn't get infected."

I poured a careful amount of water over the cut. Dylan squinted his eyes but said nothing. I groped around in my backpack, hoping the little first-aid kit was still there. It was. I pulled out a Wet One to continue the cleansing process, but Dylan shook his head, biting his lip, so I reached for a Band-Aid instead. I dried the knee with the edge of my t-shirt, and applied the Band-Aid.

"Thanks."

"Sure. Do you want to rest? Should we go back down?"

Dylan sniffed. "Turning back is for losers. If Dad knew we skipped class for this, he'd want us to make it to the top. I'm not bleeding anymore, see? Let's go."

The peak was always breezy, no matter how hot and still the ascent. Dylan insisted we all climb onto the mammoth, pink-brown boulders that huddled at the top, and I couldn't do anything but support my wounded brother. I hated heights. Not so much when there were rails or glass boxing you in – but when a gust of wind or a misplaced foot could end with you looking like ground beef on the trail, yes.

Not Dylan. He balanced as close to the edge as I could bear, and often closer.

Evan refused to budge as soon as he saw how high up we were. Jason and I, watching each other, inched over toward Dylan and together picked out landmarks: some of the other Seven Sisters, the airport with its one runway, and the California Men's Colony that sprawled, yellow, between the highway and the far mountains.

"Let's climb down the back way," Dylan said. "I want to see what's down there and I have some rope in my backpack, for the steep parts."

My stomach squirmed like I'd swallowed a gopher snake. In my most adult voice, I said, "I don't think Evan would want to go down that way."

"Well, we'll need someone to bring the rope down after us, anyway. He could hike back down the trail."

"No." I had visions of all three of us in various lifeless poses on the ground.

Dylan was breaking up our united front, but I thought I had the solution.

"We can't leave Evan to go down by himself. He'll feel bad for not coming with us."

"Well, then he should come with us."

"He hasn't been hiking very many times. He's just getting used to living here and doing outdoor stuff."

Dylan made a face, but neither he nor Jason protested. Jason looked a little less green now that scaling down boulders at the top of a mountain had been put on hold – at least more than the initial few. So we walked back to Evan and coaxed him over the edge. The crevices in between always looked bigger when you were going back down.

When we got back to the house, we were hot and sweaty and grumpy. Jason told us that his mom always said sugar made you grouchy in an "I-told-you-so" voice, although he'd eaten just as many red vines and drunk just as much soda as the rest of us.

We stripped down to our boxers in the backyard – Evan's idea, to avoid tracking dirt into the house – and drank from the hose because we were so thirsty. The vaguely mineral taste was refreshing, even though the water was warm at first. Somebody 'accidentally' pointed the hose at somebody else, and a fight ensued which lasted until we remembered that our shouting could probably be heard by everyone in the neighborhood who didn't work a nine-to-five or attend school. Dripping and shivering in the breeze that was rising as the afternoon waned, we tiptoed into the garage and cleared boxes off the dusty Ping-Pong table. We played too long, so that we barely had time for everyone to claim their clothes from the pile on the floor. Evan and Jason had to run home without the roast beef sandwiches and cartoons that had been next on the agenda.

I threw Dylan's and my clothes into the washing machine, set it to 'mixed load' and took a shot in the dark as to where to put the detergent. Dad had long ago – well, about a month after Mom left – made the call to have a housekeeper come once a week, but that meant that Dylan and I had learned very little about housework.

Dylan took the first shower and then made sandwiches with too much mayonnaise that we ate in front of the TV. Dad didn't believe in paying for television, so we had to rely on VHS tapes for cartoons most of the time. Dylan stuck in Tom and Jerry – one of those cartoons our parents had grown up watching – and I didn't object.

The wind picked up overnight and Dylan, Raquel and I agreed over breakfast that we should make the most of it. We set off right after Dylan and I gave the engine a once-over to be sure it was still in working order, in case the wind died unexpectedly further out to sea.

I was thinking about Dylan's and my expedition up Bishop's Peak again. That was the day that first set Dylan and I apart as true adventurers. There were injuries, the hearts of some of our company nearly failed them, and we barely escaped capture (i.e., discovery by our dad). After that, we read books like *Kon-Tiki* with a secret thrill of sympathy for members of 'the brotherhood'. We pored over the *Britannica Atlas*, which was old enough to show Germany divided into two halves, plotting out the expeditions we read about (Ernest Shackleton's, Captain Cook's) as well as our own imagined ones.

I never would have guessed that *this* would be the journey we finally settled on. Nor that it would be so long before we actually took the trip, nor that our reasons for going might be other than the sheer joy of exploration. Still, my youthful self would have liked the sound of Panama. The Panama Canal and jungles and exotic birds and reptiles... Come to think of it, how were we progressing along our route? Everything seemed all right on deck, so I ducked down into the cabin.

"So..." I came back up on deck to see Raquel at the wheel. "You're steering now?"

"Yeah." I guess she detected strain in my voice because she added, "Don't worry, Dylan's keeping an eye on me."

Great. Now she probably thought I was either superstitious or didn't believe women should pilot boats. When, actually... Dammit! What was my problem?

Something about the idea of Dylan teaching her navigation rubbed me the wrong way. Shouldn't that be *my* territory?

"Cool." I struggled to look unconcerned. "Oh, what I meant to say" – anything to change the subject – "was we're a little behind schedule if we're really going to make it to Panama and back before the hurricane season hits."

"If?!" Dylan's voice was louder than necessary, even in the rising wind. "Of course we're going all the way! He wanted us to go to Panama; we're going to Panama. Seems simple to me."

"Well," I looked up at the mainsail, "the wind is pretty good. Why don't we put up the jib and really get sailing?"

"Let's do it."

"Actually," I chewed on my bottom lip for a minute. What if I'd miscalculated something?

"What?" Dylan was already moving toward the jib.

"I've plotted out a course that could save us some time, but it would mean sailing farther out to sea. Out of sight of land for a while, in fact."

"If it helps us make up time, I'm down."

My eyes were on Raquel: "It will also mean sailing for about twenty-four hours nonstop. So actually, it's great that you're getting comfortable steering, Raquel."

She nodded, lips pressed tight.

We hoisted the jib, the wind freshened still more, and Raquel – with my coordinates and Dylan's instructions – set us on a course for the open sea. I stood to port, watching the brown and blonde coastline rush away with a rising sense of freedom. Then I started wondering about absent friends and enemies, like Leslie, the Rich, and Uncle Ernie back home in Solana Beach. Picking up the phone to call Dad's only brother had gotten difficult since things fell apart.

V.

It was 10 o'clock on a Saturday morning. I was drinking my first cup of coffee. My phone buzzed and I leaned over to see if it was Leslie sending me a picture of herself surrounded by tulips – her work had sent her to Holland for four or five days. But it wasn't Leslie, it was Dylan. I was so surprised, I almost dropped my phone in the sink. Dylan never texted me. Wait a minute. This was a *call*.

"Hello?"

"Hey – have you talked to Dad today?"

I stirred a little more milk into my coffee. After all these years, I still saw it as a failure that I couldn't take it black, the way Dad and Dylan drank it.

"No. Not yet. Why?"

"We always talk on Saturday mornings, and I haven't been able to get ahold of him, which is weird."

"Well, I was going to go run the Johnson trail anyway. I can drive by and see if his car's there. Maybe he forgot to tell you he left town for the weekend ...Although he didn't say anything to me either, come to think of it."

"Yeah, unlikely. Okay – just let me know."

I slid into the driver's seat a few minutes later, my heart thumping belatedly at the urgency in Dylan's voice. Down Frederick to California – why we lived so near the hub of Greek life baffled me (Stefan said it was cheaper, and I hadn't questioned his rationale – at the time). Right on California, left on Foothill, and down the long progression of lights and up the gentle incline to Patricia Drive. Bishop's Peak loomed, maternal, above our family home.

I slammed the car door. Dad's royal blue Toyota Tacoma was in the driveway, stinging my eyes as it glittered in the sun. He washed it every week, though I'm not sure when it got dirty. This truck had never been to Baja.

I let myself in by the sliding glass door at the back, which was never locked.

"Hello? Dad?"

Maybe he'd walked down to get a coffee from Black Horse – it was a mile each way, but he said it was good to earn life's pleasures. Dad was full of such aphorisms, and I could never decide whether to be annoyed or impressed at the neat little bows he sometimes liked to tie on life.

Still, it was late for him not to be back, going about his weekend routine with the garage door open and Journey on the radio. I kept walking through the rooms. The house felt too still. He usually opened a window or two around the house in the morning, but today it was shut up, dim, like a mausoleum... I thought perhaps I ought to quicken my pace, but instead I stopped moving. I had the feeling that, as long as I stood here, surrounded by the shaggy, dun-colored carpet and family pictures that predated my mother's departure, everything was all right. Dad was in the shower down the hall, or walking back with his coffee in hand, and had simply forgotten his phone call with Dylan. Not that he forgot many things, or had ever taken above a five minute shower in his life, but... time changed people. He laughed and cried more, and he moved slow on cold mornings and said his knee ached before it rained.

I checked the time: 10:15.

Dylan texted me: "???"

I forced myself down the dark hallway. All the doors were closed. I passed the door to my old bedroom, resisting the urge to go in and burrow under the covers like I was ten again and frightened by the coyotes' howling.

I came to the last door on the left – the master bathroom. I knocked. No answer. I tried the door handle: it opened. I switched on the light and sniffed. There was the woody note of the Imperial Leather soap Dad always bought. The mint green tile accosted my eyes, but no one was there. I could almost breathe easy.

The final door faced me like the maw of Cerberus. He's probably just a little behind getting his morning coffee, I reminded myself. He's not a machine. I laid my hand on the yellow metal of the doorknob, kept shiny – all but the grooves – from use.

The room lay before me, a vast desert of 'Saharan Sands' – Mom's color choice. Dad never bothered changing things after she left. Why should he? An unnecessary expense for a confirmed bachelor with two young boys. But I always wondered if there was another reason for keeping everything the same. Perhaps he hoped someday she would come back home.

I drew my eyes from the floor to the bed, telling myself I was being unreasonable and trying to calm the lurching of my stomach. The bedclothes – a haphazard mix of tan and white – Dad didn't pay attention when he took fresh sheets from the linen closet – were tousled and scrunched into a heap in the middle. I was about to release my intaken breath when I saw a hand amid the detritus of sheets and pillows.

His face was half-buried in the pillows; one fist clutched at the comforter. I felt a great quietness descend on me.

I slogged to the bedside and put out my hand: "Dad?"

I kept my hand hovering just above him. His stomach lifted the sheets slightly, but did not move up and down with his breath. I tried to force my hand down to shake him, but I could only bring myself to straighten the covers. That action alone told me more than I wanted to know. The liver-spotted hand with its fistful of covers wouldn't allow my perfunctory tidying. My fingers stopped, hands on the butter-soft sheets he would never have bought for himself.

"Dad?" My voice was crackly – adolescent.

Nothing. I blinked. Any minute, I'd wake up. Or else, I had let Dylan's paranoia mess with my head. Dad was just sick. He might be having a fit or seizure that required medical attention. I forced myself forward. I ran my mind down the list of first aid skills I possessed. Clear airways. I moved some bedding away so his face was fully visible.

His eyes stared up at mine, his mouth half open. I waited for him to make any kind of movement. Then I registered that there was no heat where my hand rested on his T-shirted shoulder. I looked again. His eyes looked so calmly back at me. Were they slightly misty? For half a second, I thought my own eyesight was failing. But as I moved to straighten his neck, to ensure his airways weren't blocked, I again felt that chill – this time skin to skin.

My flesh crawled and I jerked away – and felt an instant pang of guilt. This was the man who had gotten up countless nights with me: in the days when I still wet the bed, through numerous cases of the stomach flu, and during a time after Mom left when I had such vivid nightmares that I'd wake up screaming like I was being hacked to pieces.

But to touch him again was already taking on a new purpose: to confirm that the fear I'd spent my life *not* facing had become reality. I reached out and forced my hands to make contact with his hand: it was icy and it wouldn't unclench. My stomach heaved and I ran to the bathroom and leaned over the toilet. But I didn't throw up and I didn't cry. I just stayed there, staring into the porcelain bowl, wondering whether the lime scale from the hard water could be removed with steel wool and vinegar.

My phone rang. I started, then rummaged through my pockets. I searched every one of them twice before I realized that "Annie's Song" was coming from the other room. It was Leslie's favorite John Denver track. I walked back to the bedroom, shying like a spooked horse when I got to the door. The song stopped, and I heard the jingle of my voicemail.

I forced myself in there and picked up my phone. Should I call an ambulance? Call Leslie? My brother? Uncle Ernie? I scrolled through my contacts, feeling a comforting fog of unreality descending.

You fill up my senses, like a walk in the forest... I fumbled with the touch screen:

"Hello?"

"Why are you whispering? Is Dad there?"

I held my breath. My mind got tangled in the question: Was Dad here? His body was here. But his body didn't remember me now, though I had come from it –

"Jim – dammit! What is going on?"

"He's gone, Dylan."

"Any idea where?"

"No, Dylan, he's *gone*." I gasped as I said it. As if I were pronouncing the sentence of execution.

"Oh – " he sounded like his throat hurt. "Why couldn't he wait for me to come home?"

"I wasn't here either." The silence buzzed. "He died alone." That was it. I couldn't talk anymore or I'd be a goner.

There was a long pause on the line. Then, "I'll call Uncle Ernie. Maybe he and I can drive up to SLO together."

I nodded, then realized he couldn't see me over the phone. "Mm-kay."

"See you soon."

I wanted to ask what about the body, but I didn't want to talk any more and I was the elder brother, anyway. I should be able to figure this out.

"Okay," I said. The line clicked. I typed "mortuaries San Luis Obispo" into Google. There they were, complete with one to five-star ratings.

The first week, Dylan and I attacked the series of tasks related to Dad's death with the united front of our boyhood. Then the funeral came, and Dylan went home. I didn't really know when I expected to see him again. And now we were on the same boat with this feeling that we ought to understand each other, but we no longer spoke the same language.

VI.

"What were you like as a kid?" I said to Raquel. It was sunny, and we'd just caught some corvina on the trawl line.

Raquel looked up, her hands still holding the knife and sticky with the sweet saltiness of fresh fish. I was teaching her to fillet and she was an apt pupil.

"What was I like? I don't know...Smaller?" She laughed, setting the knife down and touching her fingers together, pulling them apart, and touching them together again.

"It's not a trick question. I'm just trying to picture you being a kid." I took up the knife she'd set aside and picked up where she'd left off with the sea bass.

She shrugged. "I guess I was a pretty happy, friendly little kid – kind of bossy, too, my brother always says."

I laughed. "That explains a lot."

"What?"

I shook my head, smiling.

"No, seriously, Jim. Tell me." Those eyebrows, when she was serious about something!

"I rest my case," I said.

She frowned; then a corner of her mouth twitched upward. "Touché."

"Tell me more about growing up. Where did you live?"

"My family immigrated to the US when I was three or four. I don't remember a lot from that age. We came for the strawberry harvest and just stayed. I do remember the house we shared with my uncle's family, Dad's brother. We lived there a couple years." She made a face. "There was always a line of dancing kids and adults waiting for the bathroom. I remember being jealous that at night the boys could duck out to pee in the backyard, but I wasn't allowed."

I grinned.

"I remember my first day of school. The teacher tried to talk to me in English. But my classmates were nearly all like me – Spanish-speaking kindergarteners whose parents were in the country illegally, mostly as migrant workers. Some people try to make me feel bad about getting a free education when I wasn't even in the country legally. I just tell them, I didn't see your parents lining up to spend all day bent double in the sun, hands in the dirt. Or pruning grapes, or cleaning toilets, or – " she paused for breath. "My point is, California needed my parents. It used them up – their youth, their vitality – and spit them out old and arthritic. They may not have paid taxes, but they sure as hell kept the economy from totally imploding."

She flushed: "I'm not trying to give you a lecture on immigration reform. I can talk about my childhood like a normal person, I promise!"

I shrugged. "It's all part of the story. Maybe this will help: happiest memory. Go."

She bit her lower lip. "Happiest memory?"

"Too many to choose from?" I stared down at the pile of iridescent fish skin and wondered how I would answer if the question were turned back on me.

"The normal amount, I guess." She pressed her palms against the worktop, a piece of plywood balanced on top of our little camp table. "I mean, as you may have gathered," she half-smiled, "it wasn't a cushy childhood. But my parents always gave us everything we needed, and as much more as they could manage. I guess, when I think about it, it's true – you don't need a lot to be happy." She inhaled, staring at the sails trembling in the wind. "Actually, the first thing that comes to mind is my family and me at the beach one day when I was probably eight. We barbequed, and I got to eat a hotdog, which I was so excited about, because we usually ate Mom's cooking. I'd kill for it right now, but when I was a kid, American junk food was such a treat... Anyway, my cousins and I played chicken with the waves afterward and took turns burying each other in the sand until the sun went down."

"Sounds like a good day."

"It was, until we got home and Mom woke us up in the dark of the car and made us take baths to get all the sand out of our ears and hair and who knows where else." She tore her eyes from the ocean. "What about you?"

I stalled. "Me?"

"Yes, you!"

"Well – "

This was supposed to be easy. I flicked through memory after memory. A minute or two passed, and I realized I had begun to smile. The memory wasn't one I would have chosen to tell, ordinarily. For one thing, it didn't seem representative of my childhood.

The setting came back in snatches. "Bennie and the Jets" on the radio. Mom and Dad in the front of the pickup, singing along – Mom's sense of rhythm notably lacking, even to my young ears. She had a big smile on her face though as she sang "B-B-B-Bennie" back at Dylan and me.

We were driving to Mom's parents' house for Christmas. It wasn't until years later I recognized that, increasingly, these trips down south were the only times I saw Mom happy. Just about the point in the drive when Dad's shoulders were folding in from the traffic, Mom perked up, like the smog and the people and the cars stretching as far along the road as I could see were some kind of vitamin boost.

"I didn't ask you to tell about your whole childhood!"

"Right. Okay. I guess I'd have to say the Christmas I was six. We were driving down to Redondo Beach to spend Christmas with my mom's family. My dad turned up the radio. Elton John was playing and they both started singing. Dylan and I joined in once we caught on to the chorus.

"We were driving past a stretch of coastline right then. I remember looking out at the winter swells exploding against the shore and thinking about the next day being Christmas Eve and the magic that entailed and feeling the impossible anticipation of Christmas morning."

I ran a hand through my hair for something to do.

"I like that," Raquel said. "Impossible anticipation of Christmas morning." Her eyes met mine and I looked away. It was an automatic response. Eye contact was just so – intimate sometimes. I looked back up a beat too late. She was piling the fish onto a plate to take down to the icebox.

At least she was pleased with my offering. I didn't tell her that that Christmas was shortly before my seventh birthday. In other words, that was the last Christmas we all spent together. I grabbed the fish guts and skin and tossed them over the side.

Nelly lurched, and I looked up from where my hands gripped the railing. The ocean had gone from moderate swells to white-toothed rollers. I looked back toward the helm. The sails shuddered as the wind switched directions. I walked as quickly as the listing deck would allow to the wheel, which Dylan relinquished gladly.

"What do you think's going on?" He looked at the clamoring seas.

I shook my head, adjusting *Nelly's* heading slightly. "Not a clue. We're making good time though. Seven knots."

"Should we reduce sail?" Raquel said.

"All good." Dylan gave her a thumbs up.

I felt a twinge of regret that we hadn't listened to the weather forecast.

Half an hour later, when the wind shifted halfway around the compass again, we were out of sight of land. We were running before the wind under full sail, close to nine knots now. The seas around us were more than choppy. If the swells got much bigger or the wind got much stronger, we could be in serious trouble. My palms got sweaty at the thought. I trusted *Nelly*, but I was less confident of her crew.

Raquel was standing beside me, watching my attempts to control the boat. "We've got to reef the sails. Tell Dylan!" I yelled. My hands were clamped, white, to the wheel.

"Reef the sails?" Dylan shouted.

"Unless you want to steer?"

"You stay here. Raquel, below decks, now."

"No!" She turned on him.

"Yes!"

"You can't make me! I'm staying here to help. I am part of this crew and I am going to do my damnedest to make sure we all make it out alive!"

"Fine!" Dylan grabbed two coiled lengths of rope and, tying one end of each to the mast, he fastened the other ends, one – with deliberation – around Raquel's waist, and the other around his own.

"See? No special treatment." Then he looked at me: "You're staying with the wheel, so you'll be all right."

I nodded, wondering if he planned to tie me up as well if I disagreed, and strangely touched at the thought.

"Okay, let's get these sails reefed before –"

In cinematic timing, the jib ripped in a gust of wind.

"Shit! Okay, we've got to work fast." He went to drop what was left of the jib and Raquel followed, moving with surprising grace along the shifting deck.

I watched them for a few seconds, then remembered that I should be focused on maintaining – strike that – regaining full control of the boat. I could feel the rudder fighting me as I tried to maneuver *Nelly* to starboard. What made me angrier and angrier the more I thought about it was, we weren't complete rookies. We should have seen this weather coming. I stared ahead, taking each wave over our gunwale like a personal insult.

"Jim! Jim! I think Dylan's gone overboard!" Raquel screamed at me from amidships.

I still said, "What?" even though I'd heard exactly what she said. My pulse thudding in my ears, I tried to separate my thoughts, which came rushing at me faster than the storm, or squall, or whatever we were caught in. I mustn't let the boat have its head. But I couldn't wait even one second to help Dylan – line or no line tied round his waist. I took off my belt and began lashing the wheel in place.

Then I looked again, and there was Dylan, dripping, but definitely not overboard, making his way towards me along with Raquel, gesticulating for me to stay where I was.

"You all right?" I gripped his shoulder to confirm the witness of my eyes.

"I'm fine – I just," he was still gasping, "got soaked by a big wave while I was on the bowsprit. We should double reef the mainsail now."

I nodded. "I think we should take a third reef." I replaced my belt and turned to Raquel. "Keep to this heading as much as possible. We'll be back."

She nodded, removing the rope from her waist and knotting it around mine. I thought about saying this was an excessive precaution, but I didn't. I could feel her fingers fumble a little as she made the rope fast. Then she placed her hands exactly where mine had been on the wheel, took a good look at the compass, and fixed her eyes on what could be seen of the horizon.

Once Dylan and I had triple-reefed the mainsail, we went below to haul up the old car tire that was our storm anchor. I was hoping we wouldn't need it, but we figured it was better to have it on hand in case conditions worsened. Our lack of sailing experience in recent years made our current situation more dangerous than it needed to be – than it would have been if Dad had been with us.

I took over steering again. Raquel rubbed her fingers to bring the blood back into them. The knotmeter showed we were doing nine knots.

"Dylan, we're not slowing down enough. I'm thinking we'd better drop the mainsail altogether."

His shoulders sloped with exhaustion, but he nodded and went forward. Raquel reattached the rope to her waist and went with him.

Dylan and I took it in shifts to sleep and steer through the night. Since Raquel was new to steering, her job was to wake up mid-shift and check that whoever was steering was alert. The pitching of the boat made sleeping difficult. By 5 a.m. we were all above decks again. No one mentioned breakfast, and I don't know if I could have kept any down. I'd barely survived my hours of 'rest' in the cabin.

By 7 a.m. the swells seemed to be diminishing and by 9 a.m. the squall had mostly abated. The only trouble was, in the stress of the weather, I had lost our heading. I approximated our position as best I could, Dylan and Raquel unfurled the mainsail, and we sailed east to find land.

The bay we anchored in sheltered us from the continuing rough seas and the worst of the wind and rain. Raquel suggested napping before we started restoring *Nelly* to her former glory.

"We've got to get the boat in shape first," I said. "As it is, we – "

"You know what, Jim? No one gives a shit about the state of this stupid boat at the moment but you." Dylan stood with his feet planted wide apart, like he was still on the open water. "We just survived a *storm*."

"I'm trying to do the responsible thing with Dad's – "

"Right. Because you're the *only* one who cares – " he stopped, opening and closing his fists. "And by 'the responsible thing' do you mean piloting us into a squall?"

I could feel my throat tighten and the hairs on the back of my neck prickling. "You know I didn't know any more about that storm – "

"Forget it, Jim," he said. "You've been in the right since the day you were born. No wonder Leslie dumped you."

Last night's nausea seemed to be returning. "What – How...?"

I felt the anger balling itself into a cold fist in my belly, but I didn't realize the fist was more than a metaphor. At least, not until I threw myself into that punch. My knuckles caught his jaw. I pulled my hand back, aching and smeared with blood – unclear whether it was his or mine. The release I felt was overshadowed by the shock that I'd actually done it. Sometimes I'd fantasized about such a confrontation with Dylan when I was white-hot angry, but in my head the single punch was impartial like the hand of Justice, and afterward we were quickly reconciled and back to our prelapsarian state.

Instead, I got a gasp and "What the hell?" from Raquel, and a yell from Dylan. A moment later, he took me down in a full tackle. The way he had me pinned, I couldn't draw a full breath. My mouth was hot and salty. I hated the taste of blood, but that was nothing to my indignation. While I lay there trying to punch, kick, and claw my way out, he pummeled my torso. He was the more muscular one, but I was more agile, and eventually I managed to wriggle out from under him, *sans* dignity. I forgot about the law of talion and went for revenge.

"Dylan! Jim! Stop!" Raquel's voice crackled with anger.

I was not about to give up a momentary upper hand, though. I slugged Dylan as hard as I could in the gut, and he gave a grunt of pain. But my own ribs were still burning, so I closed my ears and punched again.

He stayed doubled up for a minute, but Dylan was the better fighter. I might have remembered this if I hadn't been waist deep in the past by now. After another juicy jab to Dylan's face, I was unguarded. Dylan's punch laid me out.

I came around to Raquel's voice and a hellish throbbing behind my left eye.

"… unbelievable. And here I thought you were the one with a little maturity. Who is Leslie anyway?"

Could I just pass out again? My head was getting worse and I must have groaned, because I felt an ice pack slapped against the side of my head. Long hair brushed my cheek for an instant. I opened my eyes, though one of them seemed reluctant to open all the way.

Raquel narrowed her eyes: "What's your full name?"

I liked the snap of her eyes when she was mad. I guess I took too long to say something, because she leaned in and probed my left temple with her fingers. I thought about not responding to her question for just a little longer. Then her fingers found the tender spot.

"Damn! Ouch! Okay! My name is James David West."

She stood up quickly. "Well, I guess your concussion isn't too bad if you still know who you are. If you guys hadn't beat each other up so well, I'd be doing it for you right now. I mean –" she turned away with a look of disgust.

I inched my head up to look for Dylan. He was leaning against the roof of the cabin a few feet away, holding a bag of ice to the side of his head with one hand. *Crap*. He was my little brother, and Raquel wouldn't understand why I had wanted to hurt him. Not having initiated a fight since the fifth grade, I wasn't sure whether I was amazed or a little terrified at this change in myself. I guess you can't bottle anger up indefinitely.

My memory of the rest of the day is hazy. I know Raquel made us both take aspirin and hold bags of our limited ice supply to our injuries when the ice packs thawed. At one point I tried to get up and start working on the boat, but I was gripped with head-pounding nausea and vetoed that plan without Raquel having to order me back to my cot. (She'd insisted straightaway upon joining the crew that we transition to sleeping on deck.) I probably could have slept straight through from late afternoon till morning, but Raquel insisted on waking me up every few hours – allegedly to make sure my brain was okay, but it felt more like a punishment for throwing the first punch.

The next morning, Dylan was splotchy-faced and moved cautiously, but otherwise he seemed fine. Raquel went around with a frozen expression, which I think was intended to be neutral, but made me wish she'd yell at us and have done with it. For the first time since she'd joined our crew, I remembered that she wasn't contractually bound to us and could leave any time she wanted. This thought filled me with a nausea unrelated to my head's continued throbbing. Maybe a psychologist would say it was tied to the trauma of our mother's leaving. Maybe. But understanding these things seldom makes them less painful, I find.

I adjusted my ice pack and tried not to remember.

I was seven and Dylan was five and a half. I'd woken up early to check under my pillow for whatever a front tooth was worth to the Tooth Fairy. I was hoping for fifty cents. But the Tooth Fairy had forgotten to come the night before, and I came downstairs in my airplane pajamas with my tooth still wrapped in foil. No one was in the kitchen, and the cereal hadn't been set out for breakfast. But I was seven now and I knew where to find things.

I poured myself a bowl of Cheerios and put a big dollop of honey on top, getting a little honey on the table when I returned the wand to the pot. The milk would be hard to pour, so I grabbed the carton of half and half my mom used in her coffee and poured it into my bowl until some of the

Cheerios were floating on a thick white sea. I took a big mouthful. Sweet and buttery, with a satisfying crunch. Then I remembered my special spoon. I made sure I'd gotten all the honey from the grooves of the regular spoon, then replaced it with my Simba one. It had a purple lion cub's head on the end, and the spoon itself looked milky gray at room temperature. When I stuck it in cold milk, though, it turned bright orange. I was busy alternately holding my spoon in my mouth and in the milk to see it change color when I heard voices coming down the hall.

"It's too early. At least wait until the boys are awake."

Was that Dad's voice? It sounded... buried, like he was talking from underneath the house, where he sometimes had to crawl to set traps for a very persistent family of possums.

"Dammit, Dave! Do you want them to see this? It will be *so* much better for them if we just say Mommy had to go on a business trip. Then, after a couple of weeks they can start seeing me at my new place. Kids adapt. Look at us – we were practically kids when we got married."

"But that's no reason – "

"Look, if they see you like this, they'll know."

"Maybe they *should*. I don't want to lie to our kids."

I sat with my Cheerios getting soggy: I hated soggy Cheerios, but I wasn't hungry anymore. I ran my tongue back and forth over the hole left by my tooth. The skin there was soft and a little bit painful, and it almost made me forget to listen to what the grownups were saying. Then I heard Dylan's voice: "Mommy?"

I pulled myself out of the memory the way you can sometimes force your way out of a bad dream. Thinking about that day always felt like thinking about someone dead. Well, now Dad was dead – but even before that.

"Mommy" had ceased to exist for me that day, and the woman I knew now seemed like someone else's mother.

The next day, Dylan and I set to work slowly, assessing and fixing the injuries the storm had inflicted on our little craft. Raquel sequestered herself below; occasional bangs and bumps made me question whether she was clearing up or adding to the storm's damage. Not a word unrelated to the work at hand passed between the three of us.

About noon I was sitting on deck, trying to mend a tear the wind had made in our jib. The skies had begun to clear, although the wind was still howling outside our bay, and I could see a white and grey slice of sea between the hump of the peninsula and low hills of the mainland. Dylan had gone below to try to help Raquel, since most of the work on deck was done. We'd actually been lucky in the storm: our damage had been minimal – as long as the rudder was all right. We would wait until the water was less murky before diving down to check it. And it wouldn't hurt to give our injuries a little more time before diving.

Voices rose up the companionway, indistinct against the backdrop of the wind. I told myself it didn't matter what they were saying. But when Dylan's hot face and Raquel's wet one emerged, I had yet to convince myself. I pushed the folds of canvas off my lap and stepped towards Raquel. She held up a hand to Dylan and me.

"That's it. I'm done." Raquel looked me, then Dylan, in the eye, wiping away the tears with her fingers. "You guys have some serious shit to work through, and I am not going to be your psychologist-cum-anger-management therapist. And don't even get me started on how offensive it is for you to be 'competing' for me. I'm not some prize to be won."

"But we're not – "

"No, Jim. Just *listen*. I will stay till we get to Cabo because I told some friends I'd meet them there. Then I am out of here, and you can find yourselves a replacement – or not." Her voice was husky as she said it, but her eyes were scalpel-sharp as she looked at us in turn.

I looked to Dylan to lay on the charm and convince her to stay. But he just stood with his hands in his pockets, staring at the deck.

I couldn't help it; I fell back into that sour memory. Me peeking around the doorway, Dylan poised on the stairs down from the loft (where we both slept while too small to warrant bedrooms of our own downstairs). Dad's face freezing halfway into a smile, Mom – what? That was yet another reason I couldn't forgive her: I'd seen her cry every time she watched *Sleepless in Seattle*, but her eyes were almost dry as she told her own family goodbye.

"Where are you going, Mommy?" Dylan said.

I wanted to know, too.

"Mommy's – " Dad looked at her sharply and she paused a moment before continuing: "Honey, Mommy's got to go away for – for a while."

Dylan's face fell. "How long?"

"I – " she looked at Dad, "I'm not sure."

Dad's jaw clenched and then went slack. I couldn't take the suspense anymore, so I came around the corner.

"Where's your new house, Mommy? Can we go there?"

Dad muttered an unfamiliar word under his breath and turned away.

"Um – no, honey. Where did you hear anything about another house?"

"You and Dad were talking about it."

"Uh-huh." She ran a hand through her pixie cut.

Dad broke in, his voice raspy: "Your mom has decided she wants to live in Santa Barbara."

"David!" Maybe her voice did crack the tiniest bit.

"But when are we moving? What about our friends?"

"We're not moving. Just your mom."

"But what about us?"

"We're staying here. You can visit her sometimes on the weekend."

I stared.

"But you're *our* Mommy." Dylan was whimpering now.

Mom knelt down in front of him and ran a hand down his arm: "Honey, sometimes mommies and daddies don't get along anymore and they need to try something different. I will always love you, though."

She hugged him and then came to me. I clamped hands to my sides and refused to hug her back or even look at her.

She stood up slowly. "Okay. I will see you guys in a couple of weeks when Auntie Steph and I come to pack up."

Did I see tears in her eyes? Or was it just the reflection of morning light washing through the east-facing windows?

Dylan grabbed her around the waist, still crying for her not to go. I walked back to the kitchen and scooped my leftover cereal down the garbage disposal.

Mom didn't come back. My Aunt Steph came by to pick up the things Mom had listed, and the rest, she told Dad, could go to Goodwill. Of course, he never got rid of any of it.

"Jim!" Raquel and Dylan were both looking at me.

"What?" I inhaled, and the present came back. "I don't think you should leave, Raquel."

"I'm leaving. That's been covered. What hasn't been is how long it will take us to get to Cabo."

"Oh. I – I need to take another look at the charts." I gripped the handrail tight as I took the few stairs down to the cabin.

I rifled the papers on my desk, my mind spinning. This was ever my problem. The women in my life left before I had a chance to leave them.

Toward evening of that interminable day, I walked the length of the boat to where Raquel stood, staring at the ever-watchful horizon. For a second, we watched the prodigal gold and copper of the sunset.

Then, Raquel broke the silence: "So, when were you going to tell me about the breakup? Or, maybe you'd rather answer this: when were you going to tell *Dylan*?"

I shrugged. She nodded, chewing her lip.

After a pause: "*Madre de Dios*, Jim! No wonder you're such a pain in the ass. Don't you realize you can't keep crap like that inside? Your fiancé left you for another man?! No wonder you ended up punching Dylan. It's – it's not healthy. And besides, he's your brother – I thought *I* was your friend... How do you think this makes me feel?"

I fidgeted.

"Like you don't trust me, that's how!"

A couple of days – even one day – ago, I would have seized at the fragile hope in her voice, told her yes, that was right, I was just too worn out from bottling up my feelings for Leslie. Anything to tempt her to stay. But now – you could say my blood was up from the fight, or I was sickened by all the half-truths I'd been telling, or I simply no longer felt like the me of yesterday.

I looked down at Raquel, the curve of her punctuated by that still, utter strength of will, hinted at in the precise angles of her face and chest. Her long, almost spindly legs didn't seem to go with the overarching theme... I realized she was staring back up at me and I knew that I wanted always to tell her the truth.

"Look, Raquel. That's not why Dylan and I were fighting. I mean, obviously, what he said was the catalyst. But he knew anyway, and – "

She edged along the railing away from me, and I knew where her mind had gone.

"Wait. We're not cavemen. No, we weren't fighting over you!" (*Yet*, I almost added, but thought it best to keep that to myself.) "Dylan and I – we're complicated."

She pulled an *are-you-serious* face.

"Not as individuals, particularly, but as brothers. We – just – don't – get – along."

"Since when? Since always? You guys struck me as slightly less adolescent than that."

"No. I – we – grew apart." Was that it?

"Really? Then why come on this sailing trip together?"

Dylan must have walked up behind us while I was watching the sweep of the bay bob up and down to the rhythm of the waves against our anchored boat. I could sense him, even though Raquel hadn't said anything. Maybe it was his smell – the woody tang of that Monocle aftershave he wore so religiously.

"Why?" Raquel asked again. She looked at Dylan, now just behind us, with a hand in the rigging to steady himself.

My lungs seemed to lock up. Dylan was watching me.

"I thought Dylan had told you."

She shook her head, arms akimbo.

"It was our Dad's idea, this trip. But then – " I glared back at the drowning sun, "he died."

My heart was hammering against my sternum. My heart, perfectly sound and healthy, as we tend to assume hearts are, until they prove us wrong.

"What?" The snap was gone from Raquel's voice. That really showed her, Dad. Was that your plan, going and dying? To show Mom?

"Dylan? Jim?"

I said nothing.

Dylan shoved his hands in his pockets and looked away.

I went downstairs.

I stayed down in the cabin until I judged the history and condolences had alike been covered. Then I waited a little longer, and a little longer. It got harder and harder to think about going back on deck. I knew Raquel would fix me with pitying eyes – or worse, hurt eyes – and Dylan would... Actually, I didn't know what Dylan would do.

Waiting got unbearable. Probably Dylan despised me for what he might see as slinking away. My jaw tightened until my teeth hurt. Well, I *had* left him to tell Raquel about Dad's death. But he made me say the actual words.

My jawbone started to ache. I unclenched my teeth and strode around the cabin. Finally, I grabbed three bottles of Pacifico, a lime, and a knife and trudged back up on deck. I sauntered forward, popped the bottle caps, and sliced rough wedges of lime into my hand, keeping my eyes on what I was doing.

If I'd cherished a hope that pity would keep Raquel with us, I was to be disappointed. I could see that when I risked eye contact to hand her a beer. She took it and walked to the bow, presumably to be alone.

The sun was blazing orangely at us from just above the horizon as we approached Cabo San Lucas the next day. We rounded the point, and there was the harbor mouth. Dylan started the engine. I furled the sails on my own – Raquel was below, packing the last of her things.

To distract myself, I thought, not for the first time, about the mystery of presence and absence. One moment you're with someone, and your lives are one narrative, and the next, you are separated in both time and space, your two stories exist independent of each other again, and you can't share the experience of the other person, no matter how hard you try to imagine it. It isn't so different from wishing to turn back time, so you can change one thing you've done, or left undone. The irrevocability of life sometimes seems so arbitrary. We ride on this permanent forward trajectory, each of us ultimately on a wavelength shared by no other human being. I recalled, without particularly wishing to, the line in the old confession: "There is no health in us." That seemed about right. Creatures who crave eternity and companionship, but who are stuck, isolated, in temporality.

The diesel exhaust soon brought Raquel on deck. In general she had the stomach of a hardened seaman – woman – but she was susceptible to engine fumes. The pack on her shoulders made her look slighter than usual. The sight left an acrid taste on my tongue. I would say something as soon as the moment was right: if there was an instant when Dylan was out of earshot maybe, and she loosened the hard line of her mouth ever so slightly. But there never is a perfect moment for anything in life. And if you don't have the courage to take the moments as they come, you'll find yourself often disappointed.

A minute or two after Raquel came on deck, Dylan asked me to take the wheel, muttering about barometric pressure. There was nothing to be discovered by taking a reading at present: I could have deduced this from his face, even if I hadn't known anything about sailing myself. Dylan wore the exact expression I remembered seeing on his face the day I told him he was an asshole for deciding to move down to Santa Barbara and live with our mother. He descended to the cabin.

So I had my chance now. Raquel stood, one hand on the rail, her back toward me and face shaded by the sail. I wracked my brain for a smooth opener.

I coughed meaningfully. She glanced my way. I felt the words hovering around the back of my throat. They tasted bitter. I let them stay there another minute.

At last, her eyes slipped past mine, her face adamantine.

We motored into port. The warm colors of twilight seemed out of joint with the mood aboard *Nelly*, and I found myself thinking things would be easier after all with Raquel gone. Then my eyes caught on her own bottomless eyes. I'd thought there was so much time – time for questions I hadn't yet dared to ask or wonder, time for long, long silences.

We came to anchor, went ashore. I suggested drinks, but was quickly shot down with a look from Raquel. We shook hands, which was almost worse than no goodbye at all. Then Raquel shouldered her pack and walked one way down the buzzing street, which seemed all too eager to swallow her up in its market crowd, and we walked the other. Perhaps unsurprisingly, we ended up in the tackiest part of tourist Cabo. We gave up looking for a cool, hole-in-the-wall place and settled for one with reasonably cheap booze. Neither of us said it, but apparently neither of us had any intention of being sober enough for pangs of remorse tonight.

The spot we chose had a tired palm-frond roof, rust-colored walls, and Enrique Iglesias pumping through the speakers. We got a couple of beers and tried to sit far away from the single, over-eager American men in their 50s and

60s who apparently imagined that coming to a college kids' and couples' paradise would land them some hot dates. Maybe it would, after all, because I saw a few cougars eying up the pickings. I wondered how you ended up like that, living for stolen moments of romantic mediocrity.

VII.

The radio, which had been dead since Dylan and I since left Cabo, now crackled to life. Maybe we willed it back from the grave to break the heavy silence between us.

"… Hurricane has been building in the Gulf of Tehuantepec heading northwest, expected to make landfall near Cabo San Lucas. All craft within a one hundred mile radius advised to seek safe harbor. Those in Cabo San Lucas advised to evacuate if possible. If evacuation is not possible, get well away from the shore and seek shelter."

"Shit," I looked at Dylan. "Raquel – "

" – knows how to take care of herself. She's with friends. And we are no different from anyone else, Jim. We have to find a safe harbor. How far away are we from a good anchorage?"

I drew a breath in through my nose, blowing it out slowly, like instructors in those yoga classes Leslie used to drag me to said. "Well, La Paz is supposed to be a good place to wait out storms. The question is, how much time do we have? Right now, the hurricane is – what? Three hundred miles to the southeast? But if it's traveling fast, that doesn't give us long." I looked at my watch. "If we knew – "

"Hang on." Dylan turned up the radio.

"… With possible wind speeds of up to one hundred and fifty miles per hour. Hurricane Alexa is currently clocking winds of around one hundred miles per hour, and moving northwest at around thirty miles per hour. Sailors, that's around twenty-six knots for you – "

"Thank you." Dylan tipped an invisible cap to the radio.

"This speed could increase at any time, however, so we advise you not to wait. Please seek a safe location to ride out the storm immediately."

Dylan grabbed a pen and paper from below decks and scribbled. "Okay, so, if nothing changes, we have the rest of today." He wrote or doodled on the paper. "Assuming it comes straight for us. Are we that unlucky?"

I thought probably so. "I think we should go for La Paz. There's no other harbor that's half as well recommended and that we're anywhere close to."

"What? Did you read reviews on Trip Advisor about harbors to run to in case of hurricanes?"

"No… not Trip Advisor."

"Never mind. So we need to get to La Paz."

"Can you take the wheel while I chart our course?"

We exchanged places and I went below. The course was easy enough. When I told Dylan what we'd need to do, we both refrained from saying the one obvious fact. We needed Raquel. In a situation such as this, half an hour lost or gained could make the difference between getting to La Paz and *almost* getting there. The thought nipped at the back of my mind that we had signed our death warrant, Dylan and I, by losing Raquel.

But the time for soul-searching was later, or perhaps already past. Right now, we needed to make the most of the breeze. Considering that a hurricane was flying toward us, the wind was maddeningly light. I had a sense of déjà vu, but not because of our recent brush with a storm, which I knew would seem a squall by comparison to what was coming. I finally realized that I was feeling what I often felt in dreams: trying to run from some dreadful, unknown thing, my feet hardly moving, as if weighed down by cinderblocks.

An hour dragged itself along like a wounded animal. I'd seen an injured rabbit in Baja once as a kid. Its hind legs were paralyzed by a rattlesnake's venom, my uncle said. A coyote would get it, or vulture. I cried watching it, though I'd hunted cottontails with my BB gun back home (with notable lack of success). My uncle didn't have anything with him that would put the animal out of its misery. Dylan and I were the rabbits now, limping before the storm.

I looked at Dylan. He was tuning the radio, looking for conversations (in English) to get more news on Alexa. I breathed in through my nose and out through my mouth. He had the right idea. Stay focused. Don't let your mind wander into the past or the future. *Forgetting what is behind...* Gram had liked that verse.

I looked at the barometer, which I had brought up from below for the occasion. Still holding steady. Of course, by the time it plummeted, we'd be screwed. Why had we thought it was reasonable to travel down so close to hurricane season? True, this one seemed to have come out of nowhere – and unseasonably early – but even if we'd made better time, the chances of making it to safe anchorage either along the mainland or in Panama before a hurricane tore through were slim. What had I been thinking? After all, I had been the one reading most of the navigation books.

The sun blazed over the ocean, omnipresent in beams of refracted light. I could almost feel my eyes and skin shriveling. *Forgetting what is behind.* Those words stuck in my mind like a Top 50 hit. But this time they came with an image. Forgetting. I wished a single ray of radiation would slice through my memory and burn away that last, flame-tipped vision of Leslie, wrapped in a towel, kissing Stefan with her hands in his hair. It was the casual familiarity of it that hurt most. I didn't have to ask; I knew this wasn't the first time. I left the room, she left my life, but there was no leaving that memory. I'd tried. I'd even said yes to Dylan and come on this ill-fated trip.

Between turns at the wheel and adjustments to the sails, Dylan continued to scan the radio. Fuzzy NOAA updates came through at regular intervals, and cloudbursts of conversation we caught from time to time on other channels answered some of our questions about the storm. We watched the heavens for signs of Alexa, but so far, apart from slightly heavier seas, all was serene. In the map of my imagination, though, I saw a liquid darkness blooming across the water, engulfing mile after mile as the radio listed off the coordinates Alexa had reached in the last hour. The weather gurus had expected the hurricane to fizzle out in empty reaches of the Pacific, but it had veered off their predicted course while we sailed with our radio on the fritz.

The sun reached its zenith and began to decline. I handed off the wheel to Dylan once again. The wind shifted directions, so I began adjusting sail.

Dylan cleared his throat, but his voice still sounded higher than usual. "Do you see that? Back behind us?"

I shrugged before turning my head slowly to look. A few points to the east of south, a thumbprint-sized smudge obscured a section of the horizon.

"That's it. It's gotta be." There was no point dissembling.

"Shit." Dylan scratched the back of his head, then pulled at his shirt where it clung to him, dark with sweat.

"I wonder if Alexa's picked up speed since the last update?"

"No idea. But if these waves keep getting bigger, we're gonna be in trouble long before the hurricane catches us."

I tried to adjust my facial muscles into a smile, but it felt more like a spasmodic baring of teeth. "I bet nothing about this hurricane will be predictable." I made a half-hearted attempt to lighten the mood: "Who knows, maybe the waves will get smaller."

Dylan didn't smile – didn't bother responding at all. He jerked his head for me to take the wheel, then went forward and began taking in sail.

"Hey – we need to beat the storm!" I said.

"But we also need to be one step ahead of the weather – we don't have the luxury of a third crew member."

I pretended to study the position of the sun. "Fine, but don't double reef the main yet."

"Fine."

Dylan dropped the jib and reefed the mainsail, then returned to tuning the radio. A whir of static, snatches of conversation about surfing conditions in San Blas, more static, a number of stations in Spanish, and then the beeping that preceded a weather alert. My stomach clenched, but the report wasn't that enlightening. The storm was closing in, bearing down, roaring toward us – choose your metaphor. I wondered if I should say something to Dylan – something meaningful and conciliatory, before the wind got too loud.

The storm obscured more and more of the aft horizon, smudging it like someone was rubbing an old eraser over pencil markings. Back and forth. Back and forth. I started feeling queasy, and realized the waves were getting serious now. Back and forth. Stop it. No time for bodily weakness. Besides, Dylan was watching.

We seemed to move toward the land at the same speed that the storm moved across the sea behind us. But the fact was, the storm was moving much faster, and though we had exponentially fewer miles to travel, we were hampered by the amount of sail *Nelly* could carry in current conditions. The more I longed for land, the slower it seemed we were moving. The boat was sailing through oil, not water – or maybe syrup. The waves piled like snowdrifts and crashed down like avalanches around us, and sometimes on us.

The radio scraped on, although there were fewer and fewer conversations to be heard as more craft reached their desired havens.

"What if we die, Jim?" Dylan cracked a beer as he spoke.

I wanted to tell him to shut up and put down the beer and focus all his faculties on steering, since he had the wheel again, but I did not.

He kept talking. "I mean, have you ever been here before? Where you thought, 'This could be it. I could die. This is the way James David West taps out.'" He took a big swallow of PBR. "I guess the're worse ways to go. I bet Dad would have taken this any day over a heart attack in bed."

"No. What Dad would have *wanted* was not to die at 60. What he *wanted* was for us all to be sailing together without all of this shit." I gestured at the space between us, as well as to the storm behind us, lest there be any doubt. "And how come you get to be the expert on what he wanted, even though you were the one who – " I clamped my mouth shut and began to adjust the mainsail.

"Go ahead. Say it. I can tell it's eating at you."

He fixed me with his eyes. I could feel their heat even before I turned to look at him. The worst part was, there was no getting away from this. The storm was close on our heels, and the two of us were stuck on deck with this malignancy between us.

Dylan finished his can, crushing it in his free hand. "You've always had Dad on this pedestal. You spent a lot of years trying to please some idealized version of him, which didn't seem to make either of you very happy. He isn't – " Dylan's Adam's apple worked, "he wasn't – perfect, Jim."

I opened my mouth, but he kept talking:

"And Mom had her reasons for leaving, just like I had my reasons for spending my last two years of high school with her in Santa Barbara."

"You left us," my words came out with a hiss, "just like she did. You didn't see what that did to him."

Dylan nodded. "Well, maybe he should have tried to get her back. Judging from my own experience, he never asked why she left and he never said please come home."

"He shouldn't have to."

"Speaking of coming home, I came home the summer before college to see you. And you didn't want to see me."

I fumbled around on deck until I found some work to keep me occupied and away from him for a while. When I ventured back to catch what the radio was saying, Dylan threw up his hands:

"Is there anything you *won't* do to avoid talking about shit that matters, Jim?"

His hands were only off the wheel for a moment, but that was long enough for the sail to go slack. The boat lost weigh and swung broadside to the waves. I grabbed for the rigging and Dylan gripped the wheel again, just as a huge swell smacked us over till our starboard gunwale was a foot underwater.

"Shit, Dylan!" I yelled after a minute, but I couldn't stop my pulse throbbing in my eardrums long enough to think of anything more to say.

He stared ahead, forcing the boat back on course.

His silence galled me. Minutes ticked by and there was nothing for me to do but scan the radio. I turned the dial, leaving it on static until I couldn't take it, waiting for *something* from Dylan. Anything. Fine then. I moved my eyes back to the radio dial. But it wasn't fine.

"Dammit, Dylan! What do you mean Dad should have tried to get Mom back? Maybe you don't remember how bad it was when she left."

"Maybe you don't remember how bad it was *before*."

I blinked. "What do you mean?"

"The fights, the yelling. Nobody was happy when they *were* together. I think maybe he drove her out."

I stared at him. "We *are* talking about the same people, right? Dad would have done anything – he *did* everything for us."

"I think we better have the storm anchor ready," Dylan said, staring at the swells. "I can probably bring it up alone, if you can keep the bumps and rolls to a minimum."

I took the wheel. The radio, which was on a channel that had been cutting in and out, now began to play *Te Extraño*. I recognized it from the time or two Leslie dragged me along to salsa or bachata lessons, in an attempt to make me a less abysmal dance partner at weddings.

Dylan bumped around below. It seemed to take him at least two hours to bring the storm anchor up the steps, and then he still had to secure the big tire so it wouldn't roll overboard before we could deploy it. He was smudged with grease and breathing heavy.

"He would have done anything for us. Anything he could. But he couldn't – or wouldn't – do the same for her."

"What?!"

"Jim! You don't have to be so afraid of the truth."

I sucked air through my teeth. "Cut the shit, Dylan. What makes you think your version of the past is more accurate than mine? Mom got her hooks in you the way she used to have them in Dad. When you first moved down there, he'd go into your room at night and just sit there, and I'd lie in my bed next door and wait and wait until the door creaked open again."

Dylan swiped a sleeve across his eyes but said nothing.

"Why didn't he come sit with me? I lived there another year, and he never came in and just sat with me like he sat in that damn empty room."

The last sentence or two just sort of snuck out of me, and I turned away to look at the storm clouds reaching across the sky toward us. It occurred to me that, instead of a defense of our father, my words had sounded like an indictment.

The silence bled on for an eternity. The swells continued to build and the surface of each one became less like a wave and more like rough-hewn slate veined with white. The slap and slice of the boat through the rollers formed a baseline. The rigging shrilled in the ever-strengthening wind, the radio whined when we lost the signal – but still the quiet pressed down on my chest. Other silences echoed within it, detritus of the past, flung to the surface for the first time in years. I grabbed a beer, telling myself it would settle my still-rebellious stomach.

The time I had originally estimated we should be within sight of La Paz came and went – I hadn't bargained on all the weather we'd face as prelude to the storm. The sky behind us was beginning to look like I'd sometimes imagined skies to look before a tornado: mounds of black, blue, and gray cloud piled together and surging toward us.

"How much longer?"

I couldn't help laughing – my nerves craved an outlet.

"What?"

"It's just – never mind. It's not really that funny." Dylan looked like he thought I was finally cracking. "You just reminded me of every road trip we ever went on as kids."

"Okay. Now, can I get an official estimate on how far we are from port?"

"Honestly? Our speed has varied so much – "

"You don't know."

"Not exactly." I waited for the reaction.

"Okay. So how are we going to make La Paz?"

"I don't know precisely where we are, but I think we've been holding roughly to the right course."

"Okay."

"Okay?"

He shrugged. "What else is there to say?"

"I guess I thought maybe you'd say I was too busy fighting with you to pay attention to the course we were keeping. Not true, by the way."

"Jim, I believe you."

"How many beers have you had?"

"Not *that* many."

My mouth was open so wide I tasted sea spray. The boat began fighting me just then and I shifted my attention to the compass, watching the needle flutter over the mark for NW.

"What's wrong?"

"I – " I looked up. "Damn. I think the wind's changing direction again."

Dylan nodded. Neither of us bothered adding that it was getting stronger, too. Now we would have to beat to windward, which would slow our progress yet further. Dylan moved to adjust what sail we were still carrying. As I watched, a swell rose up like a cat ready to pounce. I felt a surge of adrenaline as *Nelly* plunged into its face. The rudder again seemed to resist me, and I had a brief qualm, wondering when the last time was that we'd done a visual check for compromised materials. Strange how infinitesimal choices that didn't feel like they mattered at the time could add up to be the only things that mattered.

"I think we'll make it," Dylan said.

"Would you put money on us?"

"I've always liked long odds."

My throat felt sore, and I realized we'd both been talking over the rising wind for a long time now. We lapsed into silence again.

Nelly staggered off on another tack, and I stared hard at the angry Sea of Cortez, wondering again how we hadn't thought of getting the radio fixed before we left Cabo two days ago. We were lucky we'd lingered for that extra day, spearfishing in a secret spot our uncle had told us about, or we might have been caught with no safe harbor to which we could retreat. If only we'd stayed one more day, diving in some of the little coves northeast of Cabo that looked less touristy, stocking up for the crossing to the mainland, all this might have been merely a minor inconvenience for us – something we heard about on the radio.

"Jim!" Dylan was staring off to port. I felt like someone had laid an anvil on my chest. My imagination flicked frenetically from one worst-case scenario to another.

Dylan turned around to make himself heard, but I was already staring and staring at a brownish blur on the horizon and wondering how long it had been there and what the visibility was and how much more time we had to try to reach that promised refuge.

I looked from the westering sun to the land to the hurricane's gathering mass behind us until I reminded myself of the man Hemingway describes near the end of *A Moveable Feast*, who was found buried in an avalanche, his neck worn to the bone from turning his head back and forth against the weight of the snow. For the first time, even with hope on the horizon, I believed that we could die out here.

I felt a hot rush of anger at Dad. Everything – his death, this trip, and, most of all, this storm – felt like him punishing me for something I hadn't done. I breathed heavily; the salt and vinegar smell of the sea filled my nose and mouth.

"Jim! Listen to me!"

I started.

Dylan's face was inches from mine, stubble on his chin flecked with sea foam. I felt my own unshaven jaw; my hand came away clammy. Leslie had always liked me with what she called my Viking beard because it grew out red. Then Dylan yelled at me again. I made myself absorb the words:

"Look, I don't know what's going on up here," he rapped my forehead, "but you've got to set all that personal shit to one side right now, because, *personally*, I'd like us both to survive."

I nodded. For a moment, the roles of older and younger brother were reversed, and I didn't mind.

"I think we should try to carry a little more sail. I know I was the one who wanted to reef and double reef, but I think this is our last shot at beating the hurricane."

I nodded again.

Dylan raised a little more sail, and *Nelly* strained like a thoroughbred in her paces. I corrected our heading slightly, just as there was a momentary lull in the wind. *Nelly* hesitated. Dylan and I stared at each other. We sat in the trough between two swells, the oncoming roller booming toward us. The power and brutal indifference of nature seemed bound up in that wave thundering toward us. Then the sail caught at the wind like a lung catching air, and Dylan and I breathed again.

We ploughed on through still-rising seas. It was late afternoon, but it looked like twilight was already falling. The sky was completely overcast, the clouds behind us darker than the rest. When I felt the first drop of rain, it was like the first clod of earth thrown on our boat-shaped coffin.

The contours of the land were coming into view, but its outline was soft-focus because of the rain – and would, I guessed, soon be obscured entirely. I checked our bearings and prayed that we were still heading for La Paz and not an unknown section of coast above or below it.

The sky dimmed still further and rain began to come down in earnest. I looked around. Dylan wasn't on deck. I started to get that familiar, hot-snakes-in-the-belly feeling that had dogged me since I used to lose my temper as a child. Then my brain registered the amount of water our gunwales shipped with every passing swell and I became very afraid. Before I had finished picturing Dylan overboard and *Nelly* foundering, however, Dylan's head popped up from below decks. He was wearing foul weather gear and he held another set under his arm as he made his way from one handhold to another. I yelled our heading and he took the wheel while I rammed myself into the yellow pants and coat. It seemed a futile exercise, as I was so wet already.

He looked at me, engulfed in the oversized gear: "Don't know why we didn't get these on earlier."

"You should have told me you were going below."

"Guess you didn't hear me. And you're welcome."

"I didn't know if you'd gone below or gone overboard."

"We needed this gear, Jim. Here, you take the wheel." The wind rushed into the pause. "Did you really think I'd gone overboard?"

"I – I didn't know." My throat was swelling shut.

"Not getting rid of me that easy."

I nodded and returned to watching the compass. The land was nowhere to be seen – gone, as if it had been a mirage. Maybe it had. At this point, anything was possible.

Dylan reached for the radio and held it up to his ear. After several seconds, he shook his head and slipped it into one of the oversized pockets of his coat. So we were well and truly alone.

Alone, alone, all, all alone,/ Alone on a wide wide sea.

I wondered, not for the first time, if the dead can see us. Maybe Dad was watching us right now. For about ten seconds I found this thought comforting. Then again, I might screw up and get us killed. Still, it was nice to think there was someone out there, watching our fight for life, whichever way it ended. I wanted someone to *know*, that was all. That we'd wrestled with the elements, that we hadn't just capsized in twelve feet of water. A gust sent *Nelly* quivering up the next rocky swell.

If we died, I thought Raquel might feel guilty for leaving us, but I hoped she wouldn't. We dropped into the canyon on the far side of the wave.

I wished I had called Mom last Christmas.

"Jim." Dylan was back beside me, water dripping from the midpoint of his hood to his nose and from there to his lips and scruffy chin.

"What?"

He just stood there looking at me.

"What is it, Dyl?"

"I don't know if we're going to make it."

"We have a decent shot."

"Let's be honest, Jim."

I couldn't tell if he was angry; we had to shout all the time now and the rain was streaming into my eyes as fast as I blinked it out.

"That's why – I need to – I wish – " I could see his cheeks puff as he expelled a breath, "I think he knew, but I just wish I'd told Dad. And I don't think you –"

I jerked back at the word "Dad." Dylan's face sagged. I guess he hadn't finished what he was going to say. I looked at my watch. Time to come about. I put the wheel over hard. I glanced over, half expecting Dylan to be gone, but he was still there, watching *Nelly* fumble for her footing again.

"Okay," I yelled finally. "What is it, Dylan?"

Dylan met my eyes, looked down, then back up. He yelled across the wheel: "Dammit, why isn't this easier?"

I shrugged. The gesture felt drowned inside the huge coat. "What? What is it, Dylan?"

"Well, hell." Dylan's hand whitened around the rope he was gripping. "I love you, Jim."

"You too," I said without thinking. Then I thought for a minute and realized it was true, whatever else might also be true. I watched the needle of the compass and thought some more. "You're not just saying that because we might die?"

"Damn straight I am. Otherwise, wild horses, etcetera. But that doesn't make it less true."

I nodded. The rain and cloud had locked us in now, and we were sailing blind. Since the radio had gone quiet, we didn't even know how far behind the real storm was. That made my stomach turn: this was still just the prelude.

I wasn't sure I was ready to die. Like most, I accepted mortality academically, but when it came to that moment of "I could actually die," I clutched denial like a life preserver.

I'd noticed a while back that we were riding lower in the water. We might be heeling too far over and taking on more water than washed back out through the scuppers. But *Nelly* was shipping too much water even after Dylan adjusted the sail. A leak below was the other prime explanation, but I refused to consider it. Dylan and I both had to be on deck to handle the boat. The leak just *couldn't* exist.

My stomach hurt. I wasn't sure if it was nerves, hunger or seasickness. Dylan and I had sailed for hours now without even a drink of water, just a beer or two, and that didn't really quench your thirst like you hoped it would.

The time we'd had our first beers used to be one of Dylan's favorite stories to tell. From time to time when we were growing up, Dad would buy a six-pack of PBR and stick it in the freezer to get cold before the game (usually football, but occasionally hockey).

One time, just as the game was getting interesting, Dylan slipped and fell off the roof of our tree house, from which I'd bet him he couldn't see down into our neighbor's living room. He later claimed he'd seen them watching *Jurassic Park,* and I countered that he couldn't possibly have been up there long enough to know that.

Anyway, somehow Dylan was okay, except for a sprained wrist – so the doctor informed us after a four-hour wait in the ER and a pricey X-ray. By the time we got back, the game was long over, we were all starving, and Dad's beer supply had frozen and exploded in the garage freezer. Showing remarkable calm, Dad sent us inside to watch cartoons and eat Pringles while he emptied the freezer – and possibly vented his frustration – in peace.

The next day was Sunday, and we woke early, as kids who are under ten sometimes perversely do on weekends.

Going out to inspect the scene of the disaster (Dylan's arm, not the beer explosion), we discovered the PBR cans sitting in a residue of beer and water in our Red Flyer.

The beer cans looked a lot like soda cans. Did beer taste like soda? Why weren't we allowed to drink it? Was it too full of sugary goodness? I was on the fence, but Dylan insisted that we ought to try it. We owed it to our less fortunate, less experienced friends. Maybe Dad had left the cans out here for us.

Curiosity trumped my scruples, and we each took a beer in hand, trying to look like we knew what we were doing.

I counted to three and we drank at the same moment, Dylan holding the can in his one good hand. The beer was flat and I didn't like the sour tang of it. I started coughing and spluttering, but Dylan (except for a grimace) kept his cool long enough to swallow a manly gulp. Not wishing to appear the weaker one, I forced down the rest of mine in sips and swallows – mainly while holding my breath. I'm not sure, but I bet they were only half or three-quarters full apiece. Dylan of course finished his. Then we went in to have breakfast. Dad found us both on the couch an hour later, fast asleep.

Maybe he smelled the alcohol on our breath. Maybe he went out to throw away the cans and found the empties. Maybe it was fatherly intuition. Anyway, he knew. We were woken up and made to run laps in the neighborhood until we confessed – or threw up, in my case. Then Dad sat us down on the couch for a talk about his friend Tom, who had had a college football scholarship all lined up, but blew it when he started drinking his last year of high school. He still cleaned the locker rooms at the same high school and earned just enough money to feed his addiction. We were suitably shocked at how close we had come to sharing Tom's fate. In retrospect, I wonder whether Tom was an amalgamation of Dad's fears for us with a few memories from his own past.

Of course we still told our friends we'd tasted beer, and of course we commanded a certain respect as a result, but we also respected alcohol from then on – at least until high school, when our paths diverged there as elsewhere.

Once I'd thought about being thirsty, I couldn't stop. It took me nearly two minutes of dry mouth and aching throat before I thought to tilt my head back and stick out my tongue and catch some of the waterfall from the sky. The rain also ran into my eyes and nose and down my neck, but the partial relief was worth it.

Dylan climbed up the pitching deck toward me. He had to get almost nose to nose with me before I could hear him: "Dude, this blows. We should at least be drinking the rest of the beers if it's our final our hour, but they're below. I don't want booze to be the reason we don't make it. Although, people have died for worse reasons."

I nodded. I didn't feel like yelling back.

"Want me to take the wheel? You look super tired."

I was tired. My arms, now I thought about it, were stiff, the nerves, cords of fire. A vein behind my left eye had begun a pulsating bass. My back was a growing collection of knots. Yes, I was tired. I should let Dylan take the wheel and quit putting our lives at greater risk than necessary. But –

Dylan pried my fingers free and stepped into my place: "I've got this, Jim. We'll be fine." But I didn't feel fine. Quite apart from the impending hurricane, my stomach was feeling worse and worse.

At last, in desperation, I left Dylan at the wheel and went below in search of our first aid kit, which had some seasickness pills in it. Below decks, everything that wasn't tied or nailed down was scuttling across the cabin. Gallon jugs of water, pillows, maps, cans of beer, a couple of onions, all slid from one side to the other and back again as the slope of the floor shifted. The kit was nowhere to be found, and I regretted my decision to venture into this airless space.

Ten minutes later, back on deck, I felt my will losing the battle with my body. I made a lunge for the side and let it all out. I was staggering back to my feet, my face cascading sweat, when I realized Dylan was shouting at me. I couldn't understand what he was saying or gesturing about. Too late, I realized he was warning me to look out for the boom. It caught me in the back of the skull with a dull thud that echoed inside my head. I found myself laid out on the deck, my eyes watering. After a minute I struggled up. Dylan was beckoning to me from the wheel, so I made my way over to him. As I opened my mouth to say something, I realized that my lips were wet. I licked them and tasted blood.

The next glimpse I had of land was so shadowy I told myself it was a marriage of my imagination, which had been acting strangely since that blow to the head, and the fading light. But then I saw brown again and squinted hard for confirmation – if it would just stay in view for two seconds at a time! I didn't think I had any adrenaline left, but somehow the vein behind my eye began pulsing faster and, as we crested a wave, I saw behind the dark of the rainclouds the heavier dark of two hills pressing their way through the weather. We were close to land – much closer than I had dared to hope – and as I tried to point it out to Dylan, off the starboard bow, I realized that we were coming in awfully fast.

Dylan whooped and turned the wheel back over to me as the slightly more experienced navigator. I chose not to bring up the fact that ever since my close encounter with the boom, my head had felt like it belonged to someone else.

Dylan leaned toward me to shout something, but the wind snatched it away. The next wave's break was more pronounced than the last, and my heart floated up in my chest. As we slipped down, Dylan grabbed my arm and pointed. I didn't see anything.

He put his mouth to my ear and yelled: "There's a boat."

"What? Where?"

"Looks like it's foundering."

"Where?"

We pitched to the top of the next swell and seemed to settle there.

"Dead ahead!"

By then, I didn't need Dylan to tell me. He grasped the rigging as he made his way forward to try to strike the sail. I wished, not for the first time, that I'd thought to rig us a line to hold onto before we hit this weather, or that we'd repeated the slightly juvenile but effective fix of tying ropes to ourselves for safety. Only this time, the boat herself might not protect us. I tried and failed to adjust our course. It felt like we were still suspended at the top of a wave with our stern out of water, though in fact we were fighting our way up another roller.

The view before us was a dismal one. Although rain still veiled shoreline, an arm of the land reached around protectively. Just outside, from what must be the high point of a sandbar, an orange and white shrimper pointed its wing-like apparatus toward the sky. We pounded down another wave, the wind driving behind us as I tried to steer us on a course to one side of the foundering craft.

Dylan held the flare gun. He fired one flare over the vessel. An orangy pink tail of light cast a glow over the Dante-esque scene.

"What are you doing?"

"Finding out if anyone's still aboard."

No answering flares glanced off to skyward. But when we saw the boat again at the pinnacle of the next wave, a figure clung to the shrimping tackle with one arm, waving wildly at us with the other.

"Now what do we do?"

"Do you think the harbor patrol – ?" Dylan stopped. "Nobody else will be out, with the hurricane about to hit."

I shook my head. That left *us* to try to save whoever was on the stranded vessel. And we had no guarantee of making the harbor ahead of Hurricane Alexa, even without this complication. I tried to see the map again in my head, but my memories were all a little fuzzy at the moment. Were we seeing the peninsula that, according to the charts, formed one half of the narrow mouth of the La Paz Marina? I couldn't be sure.

Around us, each swell looked like a shark's mouth, ribbed with shiny white teeth. The gray of the sea and sky was infinite. The wind's howl leapt to another pitch of intensity. When I looked ahead again, the rain momentarily (I hoped) obscured all, and the rudder now definitely refused to move us to right or left. Though I couldn't see, I knew we still ran towards the shore at an angle that set us on course for a collision with the shrimper. Now that we were running under bare poles, the sea would send us in the path of least resistance. Time alone would tell us what that was. I felt what was left in my stomach roil, but I swallowed hard and kept my eyes fixed ahead.

The wind switched directions again. I jogged the wheel; still no response. Dylan kept staring alternately at the storm anchor, then the zodiac. I knew the questions that were swirling through his head: how to control our direction, how to rescue the man on the shrimper without running aground ourselves, whether any of us would make it out of this alive. I looked again at the man, roosting in the skeletal branches of that boat, and wondered how he'd gotten himself into a worse situation that we had.

"He has to jump."

"What?"

"He has to jump clear of the wreck – that's the only way we can get to him. If I take the zodiac in, you can stand off to port until I pick him up."

"The wheel's not working," I said.

"I know. We'll use the storm anchor to help control our direction."

"That's assuming we don't run him down first."

Dylan nodded.

"How will you get him to jump?"

"Wave frantically, I guess."

A wave caught us and flung us into the next gulf. When we came up again, the shrimper was just ahead of us and a little to our right.

"We have to take the chance." Dylan indicated the storm anchor, which we'd put off using in our rush for safe harbor.

I (rather pointlessly) lashed the wheel in place and went to help Dylan. We launched the anchor and then unlashed the dinghy and removed its engine cover. Dylan and I looked at the waves.

"Are you sure – ?" I meant to say *don't you dare do this*, but the gulf between my mouth and my mind seemed greater than usual.

"Yep."

I grabbed my side of the dinghy. We dropped it down and I watched, holding onto the side to keep my dizziness in check, as Dylan jumped in the dinghy while *Nelly* hung in the hollow between two waves.

I opened my mouth twice before I could make the words come out. "*¡Vaya con Dios!*"

I unfastened the painter and tossed it to him, then watched him yank the engine cord. I couldn't hear if the motor was starting or not. But he kept pulling at the cord and another wave surged forward and I finally wondered why I had to be the one to stay with a boat we couldn't steer. The oncoming wave was plummeting down in a fury of spume when the zodiac finally shot forward and over the next swell, making for the boat on the shoal.

I checked our heading and speed. We were running before the wind, but our speed was beginning to slacken. Good. I glanced at *Nelly*'s engine – it was still covered, so there was a chance it was in working order if we needed it later. We might have enough diesel to motor in once – if – we reached lighter seas closer to shore. For the moment we were fortunate – the wind was driving us perpendicular to the waves, not broadside to them. But what if that changed?

I looked toward Dylan. He was bouncing off the swells like a Ping-Pong ball. I kept my eyes on him like they could will away the monstrous waves, but slowly my vision blurred and the scene was overlaid with another from our past... the first time I'd truly been scared for his life.

I woke from sleep. I thought I'd heard a noise in the bathroom, so I made my bleary way down the hall and flipped on the bathroom light. Dylan lay sprawled across the floor, eyes closed, the front of his t-shirt covered in vomit that matched the peach of the tile.

I knew where he'd been and I knew what he'd done – in rough terms, anyway. Since I was the follow-the-rules-and-hedge-your-bets older brother, I had only ever drunk to the point of getting a buzz. That was more for the courage it gave me to talk to girls, and to silence those who questioned my manhood, than because I liked the taste or the soft-focus grip on reality that came with consuming alcohol. I'd always found excuses to leave parties early, and I guess I'd expected Dylan to do the same.

But this had been a party Dylan was invited to on his own. Dylan, whose growth spurt and coordination had allowed him to join the football team this year, had recently informed me that my friends and I were class-A nerds. Apparently, no one invited a nerd to the real parties, even if that nerd's brother – who was awfully young to be a sophomore in high school – was in with the cool crowd.

But that wasn't important now. Now, looking down at my fourteen-year-old brother's still body, I was mad – all the more so for being desperately afraid. How much had he drunk? Maybe he had alcohol poisoning – the kind you read about in *The Telegraph-Tribune*, Cal Poly freshmen a few years older than me dying in fraternity initiations. I inched toward him, then back to lean on the sink, then forward again. Sweat from my armpits ran down my ribcage.

"Dylan!"

No answer.

I prodded him with my bare toes.

Nothing.

Dad was at a trade show, and he'd forgotten to call and tell us the hotel he was staying in. Our family still didn't carry cell phones. Hell, it had been a struggle to convince

Dad we needed the internet. I'd have to make the judgment call on my own, with all of my fifteen-and-a-half years of wisdom. I bent down and put my index and middle fingers to Dylan's jugular. Still moving blood.

I grabbed a washcloth, wet it at the sink, and laid it across his forehead while I argued with myself. Calling 9-1-1 was a last resort – Dad had always impressed that upon us. He was self-employed, so our health insurance was minimal, and an ambulance ride was a luxury we couldn't afford unless someone was dying. Plus, Dylan would get busted for underage drinking. But he might die. I was taking shallow breaths that didn't really feel like breathing.

I held my breath against the smell and leaned closer: "Dylan? Dylan!"

Nothing.

I slapped his face, hard.

His eyelids fluttered up: "Hey bro! What's up?"

I breathed again, and instantly regretted it. "How much have you had to drink?"

"Mhgmmm – " He heaved and reached the toilet just about in time.

After a minute, I said, "Stay here." Unnecessary, as he was still hanging onto the toilet bowl. "I'll be right back."

I ran to the living room and typed "alcohol poisoning" into the computer, my fingers punching half the keys wrong. I scrolled through the symptoms – twice, because I read down the entire page the first time without taking in a word. No, he seemed to know who I was, he wasn't (still) unconscious, he wasn't having seizures – or was he? I ran to the bathroom. He was snoring on the floor, an arm extended around the porcelain base of the toilet.

I inhaled slowly, watching Dylan's chest pumping up and down. Then I marched to his room and grabbed a shirt and jeans from his floor at random. So he wasn't dying. In that case, the prick was gonna hear about this from Dad. Soon. I grabbed some Gatorade from the fridge and stomped back to the bathroom to fix him up.

When I saw Dylan walking towards me the next evening, I knew he'd talked to Dad. His lips and eyebrows were bunched together, and his shoulders had that aggressive stoop usually reserved for bullies. I braced myself, my heart thumping harder at the thought of a fight.

But when he got to where I stood, looking as carelessly as possible across our yard to the lavender mountains that had once held fire, he knocked into me hard with his shoulder and kept walking. *So this is the way it's going to be.* I felt the adrenaline evaporate. I watched him walk past our long-neglected tree fort and push through the back gate into the dry grass of the hillside we'd played on even before our school-ditching days.

Half of me wanted to run after him and explain that I'd ratted on him for his own good. But it had also given me a twisted pleasure to point out Dylan's Achilles heel to Dad – Dylan, who had been scouted by the football team, dated the prettiest girls and still somehow managed to pull all As... Even as I'd described the odor of alcohol that had drenched Dylan's shirt, I kept hearing "Hey bro!" and seeing Dylan's eyes on me, so trusting – the same look he'd given me when I'd taught him how to ride a bike without training wheels. But the damn words had come out, and Dylan was grounded for a month.

I didn't go after him that night as he walked into the dusk. When I realized a few days later how untenable the situation would be for us and attempted to apologize, Dylan informed me that I was a real bastard and I'd be lucky if he ever trusted me again.

After that, I noticed the way Dylan came thirstily back to Dad whenever he'd accomplished something, hoping the disappointed look had gone. Of course Dad forgave him, and of course I felt like the one who'd been cheated on both counts. It took months to begin repairing the breach, and then, when Dylan finished sophomore year of high school, he decided to move down to Santa Barbara to live with Mom and play for a bigger high school football team.

I floated back to the present, where the waves were still slyly increasing their break. I could tell from the ever-more-perfect right angle of the shrimper with the sea that it would not be long before it was broken up and absorbed into the deep. Dylan had – it seemed to me, miraculously – managed to bring the zodiac almost directly beneath the man and was waving with his free hand for the man to jump. But the figure did not budge. I cursed him inwardly. This was his window, and if he didn't change his mind he was lost – and every second he kept Dylan there, Dylan was spinning closer to the same fate.

A fierce gust of wind sent *Nelly* flying forward and threw me off-balance. I caught at a halyard and held myself as steady as I could, searching the waves to starboard for the dinghy. I couldn't see it above the swell. The stranded vessel, though, I could see. A second gust of wind caught at the shrimper and shook it like an apple tree. The man had no choice now. He dropped into the writhing, dark sea and my eyes lost him as another breaker rolled through.

The trough I was in hollowed itself out and the wave folded down over the boat in a fountain of saltwater. Even with my foul weather gear on, rivulets of water ran down my neck. I strained to catch sight of Dylan, but to no avail. To make matters worse, the remnants of daylight that had been sifting through the storm clouds were dwindling down to nothing. I felt as though my blood stopped pumping, solidifying in my veins as I realized it would soon be too dark to see the zodiac at all.

I could at least give Dylan a chance of finding me, though our little navigation lights wouldn't be much use once the hurricane hit. It felt like Alexa should be here by now – this was a cosmic intake of breath before the release that sent us all into the ocean's long, cold embrace. I slogged forward to switch on the lights. One blinked to life. The other two, despite promises of weatherproofness, seemed to have succumbed to corrosion. Damn this crummy old boat.

At the top of the next swell, I looked to starboard and there, ricocheting off the steep slope of a wave, was my brother. The dinghy was fleeing an oncoming wave, but from that peril was flying into the path of the sailboat.

My brain seemed to slow down time so that I could absorb every agonizing feature of the scene unfolding before me. The clean line of *Nelly's* prow, illuminated by its single light, against the umber cast of the sea. The orange stripe of the shrimper slowly slipping out of sight, its lights glowing like stained glass as they hovered just below the surface, until its spidery tackle at last disappeared and the whole was inhaled by the waves. The purpling sky behind me. And the scudding zodiac getting doused – I sucked in a salty breath. They hadn't beaten the last roller. I clutched the life preserver I held ready to throw to Dylan and tried to quiet my spinning head. *Commend their souls to the deep* shuddered through my mind. *Nelly* slipped on toward the site of the zodiac's last disappearance.

"Jim!"

I don't know if I heard a yell or somehow *felt* him call my name. I looked to my right. There was the zodiac, its bulbous sides shedding water. Dylan and the other man were still inside, their bodies streaming water, too. I waited for Dylan to throw me the painter. He looked at me, blinking the salt out of his eyes. I held my hands at the ready, but still he waited. I shouted something about his having a death wish, knowing full well there was no way he could hear me. Then, as the next swell lifted the zodiac, he aimed and threw the painter right between my hands. Moments later, they tumbled aboard. Dylan and the man from the shrimper lay on the deck, breathing hard and choking up saltwater.

With our zodiac safely stowed again, I had leisure to wonder about our new passenger. It was still an open question whether we had in fact rescued him or only prolonged his cat-and-mouse game with death. Another wave crashed down on us, and we all clung to what was nearest as seawater swirled around the deck and sloshed out of (or over) the gunwales. Dylan picked his way toward the slumped figure by the mainmast, pulling himself along from handhold to handhold. I followed.

"I think he just passed out," Dylan said. "Let's get him into the cockpit."

I nodded. We inched along with him between us, clinging to every handhold along the way. I kept my eyes squinted to keep out salt water, also to try to keep the deck steady. For some reason it kept spinning in front of me. When we at last heaved our burden into a corner of the cockpit, Dylan grabbed a length of rope and began to tie him in place. The man stirred, but he put a hand on Dylan's and shook his head when Dylan moved to untie him. He gestured at the sky and said something neither Dylan nor I could hear, let alone understand. I wondered if he thought we ought to lash ourselves similarly, a trio of Odysseuses preparing to hear the sirens' song. I didn't know what could be worse than the weather we were experiencing, but I imagined the gale force winds at our heels would soon enlighten me.

Dylan I would have tied up too, if I could, but he kept up a fever of movement, as unwilling as I had been to accept our powerlessness with the failure of the rudder. We tried to adjust course with the sea anchor, but as it was a car tire, and no high-tech model, it didn't seem to have any measurable impact. Dylan shouted something about the storm jib, but both of us knew it wouldn't be enough to control our heading either.

At this moment, for some reason, Billy's parting shot flashed through my mind. Lucky I didn't believe in curses. I shoved it away and extended my hand to Dylan.

"You want to hold my hand?" Both of Dylan's hands still firmly gripped the useless wheel.

"I was going to shake it."

"Oh." His hand grasped mine. "Now what?"

I shook my head.

Just then, a torrential wave drove into us from one side. I struggled to fathom what this could mean. As *Nelly* fought to right herself though, there was a sudden hush. Dylan and I looked at each other. I peered ahead, hardly daring to think the thought in my mind until my eyes confirmed it. But it was true. We were, at last, within the protection of the land. We did not experience much immediate relief from the waves. Massive piles of water still flung us about, but for the moment I did not care. We had made it to La Paz. Well, almost. We were nearing the harbor.

After the initial euphoric relief wore off – expressed for all of us by the shrimper crewman's, *"Gracias, Señor"* – I remembered that I had no way of guiding us into the harbor and that Hurricane Alexa was still on her way.

"Dylan." I wasn't shouting for the first time in hours, and my voice sounded splintered. Maybe it was distorted by the roar of the weather just beyond the reach of the land, or maybe this was all that was left of my vocal cords.

Dylan turned his head.

"How are we going to steer?"

His eyes were blank. My stomach dropped. We could yet be wrecked, here, within sight of land. If *Nelly* managed to maintain this course without our help, we should make it. But if it changed substantially...

Dylan turned to the man still huddled in the corner.

"*¿Tu hablas Ingles?*"

"*Sí.* Yes." The man looked at us, asking no explanation for our desertion of the steering wheel.

"What's your name?" Dylan said.

"Cristóbal."

"*Mucho gusto*, Cristóbal. I'm Dylan, and this is my brother Jim."

We exchanged nods. It was nice to know the name of the person you might die next to.

"We have a small problem," Dylan said.

I resisted the urge to laugh at this understatement.

"We can't steer – our rudder is broken."

Cristóbal remained silent for so long, I wondered if he was in shock. Finally, he said: "Do you have – *como se dice* – a pole, like this," he indicated the dimensions with his hands, "and some wood pieces?"

Dylan and I stared at each other. Clearly neither of us had expected those particular words to come out of his mouth. Dylan squinted his eyes: "I think so, somewhere in the cabin."

"It will not be easy, but if you are able to – "

Dylan's eyes lightened suddenly: "We can jury-rig a rudder!" He was down to the cabin and back before I had time to figure out how this was going to work. He began assembling the equipment.

"Do you really think –?" I said.

"Do we really have a choice?" He handed me and Cristóbal headlamps that he'd found below. Good timing, too, as it was getting inky dark.

We knelt together to work. Three pairs of hands were, it transpired, one pair too many, so after a few minutes I returned to the helm to keep watch. What we'd do if I spotted an obstacle ahead was unclear.

The waves and the wind, which the land so far was unable to defend us from, drove us onward through the encroaching night. If I closed my eyes, I could almost convince myself I was on a ride at a theme park, complete with groaning timbers and eerie darkness and showers of cold water.

A shout blew toward me. I turned, barely able to make out what I saw through a sudden squall of rain. Relief flooded in when I counted two headlamps still on deck. A moment later, Dylan came forward.

"Pretty sure we've done it!"

I couldn't think of what to say, so I just breathed.

"We won't know for sure till we try it out."

"Okay."

"Want to pilot us in?" Dylan said.

I took my belt off the steering wheel, the boat dipping and rising with swells that heralded the storm. The harbor lights beamed out towards us like the welcoming arms of a mother. I steered as in a dream. I was once again Odysseus, this time guiding his vessel between Charybdis and Scylla; I was Charon, rowing dead souls across the Styx; I was Ahab, leading his crew in search of a monstrous white whale...

I caught myself as my eyes blinked shut. No. I would not shipwreck us so close to safety. Judging by glimpses of the flickering lights on the buoys, we were in the channel between the little peninsula and the heart of the city of La Paz. The waves were shrinking now and the wind was almost a breeze in comparison to what it had been. To say I was anxious to get us ashore would be a massive understatement, and I eagerly agreed when Dylan suggested using the motor. Unbelievably, it caught. We were just rounding the peninsula into the haven of the bay when I was shocked out of my cautious optimism.

It is one of the few times in my life I would say I indisputably had an intuition – I *felt* rather than saw that there was something ahead of us. The rain was thickening the already dark air so that I could make out very little, apart from the blinking lights guiding us into the harbor.

"Did you see that?" I turned to Dylan, who was standing behind me.

"No – where?" He sounded as tired as I felt.

"It's right – " I willed my eyes to see past the dim glow of our lone navigation light.

Dylan disappeared. I refrained from getting irritated, mainly because that would require more energy. A moment later, I heard a click and a tail of pinky-orange flame burrowed into the blackness. A glare of light burst overhead, reflecting in the water and into my eyes.

Cristóbal crossed himself in the bow. Then I remembered to look for what the flare should be illuminating. In what felt like hours but was probably a few seconds, I took stock of the sweep of water ahead of us.

Dylan cursed softly. It must have been a ketch – not much smaller than our own vessel. But evidently its pilot had neither luck nor knowledge of the La Paz harbor on his side. All that was visible now were the bow and part of a tattered sail clinging to the mainmast. I hoped the crew had abandoned ship in time, and I wondered whether I would have managed to steer us clear of their fate, had Dylan not fired that flare.

The wild night closed in yet again, and gusts of wind reminiscent of the open sea began to sweep in at regular intervals. The hurricane. I adjusted our course and opened the throttle on the motor.

In *The Log from the Sea of Cortez*, John Steinbeck and his travel partner Ed Ricketts tell of La Paz as they observed it in 1940:

Everyone in the area knows the greatness of La Paz. You can get anything in the world there, they say. It is a huge place--not of course so monstrous as Guyamas or Mazatlán, but beautiful out of all comparison. The Indians paddle hundreds of miles to be at La Paz on a feast day. It is a proud thing to have been born in La Paz, and a cloud of delight hangs over the distant city from the time when it was the great pearl center of the world. The robes of the Spanish kings and the stoles of bishops in Rome were stiff with the pearls from La Paz. There's a magic-carpet sound to the name, anyway. And it is an old city, as cities in the West are old, and very venerable in the eyes of the Indians of the Gulf. Guyamas is busier, they say, and Mazatlán gayer, perhaps, but La Paz is *antigua*.

We couldn't have commented much on this description when we arrived: it was dark – both with night and storm. *Nelly* was being slammed by waves that would have frightened me, had I not just escaped a storm that I knew spelled death. At the same time, we were trying to approximate an anchorage near to shore, where perhaps *Nelly* would also have a chance of riding out the storm.

To this day, I'm not sure how all three of us made it ashore alive. Our little headlamps and the navigation light at the bow seemed to amplify the all-eclipsing blackness. Still, we not only made it off the heaving sailboat into the zodiac, but all the way to the beach. True, we overshot the mark by a few yards and the propeller ended up chewing sand. I shut off the motor and we stumbled along a few feet further, dragging our zodiac, then we wedged the propeller back in the sand and ran toward a faltering patch of light.

It was a *cantina*. Possibly its proprietor was a devotee of Saint Christopher, who is said to have extended mercy toward travelers in extremity. In any case, the door latch was easily lifted and the wind, like the hand of God, shut the door of the ark in which we would ride out the hurricane.

Inside, a radio sputtered, shifting between Prince Royce, *mariachi*, and what I guessed from a few key words and their official cadence were weather alerts in Spanish. The wind screamed into the room through imperfect joins between door and doorframe, window and windowframe. Aside from the lights and radio, the place showed every sign that its owner had been prepared for Alexa. No glasses were to be seen and only a single, nearly empty bottle of Patrón remained on a wooden shelf. Hands shaking, Dylan grabbed it. He motioned to me and Cristóbal, and the three of us huddled on the floor behind the bar, watching the lights flicker and listening to the wrath of the storm and passing the bottle of tequila back and forth. I stared at wedges of lime and crushed chips and a few cockroaches on the floor and wondered what Dad would make of us now. I looked at Dylan, who had the bottle again, and smiled weakly.

He raised the bottle: "To life!"

As we expected, it was not long before the lights (and with them, the radio) went dark. Even though I was prepared for the blackout, and even though our headlamps were still working, my stomach knotted and my hands grew clammy when the night dropped around us.

The storm shook us like dice in a cup. Time began to feel elastic again, stretching moments into infinity. I wondered if, like Billy Pilgrim, I was getting "unstuck in time."

I don't know when exactly I realized that Cristóbal was nowhere to be seen. I hadn't heard him leave, but at some point he just wasn't there anymore. Later on, when I asked Dylan about that night, he didn't remember a man named Cristóbal at all. Perhaps he had been our own patron saint, or guardian angel, sent to guide us safely to La Paz.

I looked over at Dylan, but he was snoring in the corner. *Sleeping for sorrow.* Maybe that was the way forward, but between the storm and my still-throbbing head, I couldn't sleep. In the end, I started to let the past back in because I couldn't bear my own lonely silence anymore.

In memory, I'm five again, and tomorrow is the first day of kindergarten. I'm looking at a book, already feeling very grown up in my new status as student, but also wishing I could play zoo with Dylan and our rubber animals. He calls my name from the living room floor, wistful. Unable to resist the temptation if I stay, I carry *Andy and the Lion* into the kitchen, where Mom and Dad are. I take a seat at the table and turn each page slowly, focusing on the words instead of the pictures, trying to piece together the letters I know. I glance up after a minute, wondering if they've noticed my reading. But Dad's face is buried behind sheets of newspaper and Mom still stands facing the sink, although all the dishes are done. I wonder why nobody says anything. Mom turns around when the hall clock chimes eight. Her eyes look hot, like she's been rubbing them a lot.

"Okay, Jimmy, time for bed."

I glance at the paper, but Dad says nothing. Then I lay in bed and feel like crying, though I'm not sure why.

Then, unavoidably, I am transported to a late fall morning, cool and serene, and to Leslie and I hiking up the Avila Ridge Trail to look out over the iron blue Pacific and the shoreline stretching from Grover Beach – maybe even Lompoc – all the way along Pismo and Shell Beach and on to Avila, Port San Luis, and a corner of the land belonging to the Diablo Power Plant.

I said something trite, like how peaceful it was or how much I loved the ocean, and waited for Leslie to continue in a similar vein. But she just kept quiet, and I looked away from the view. She stood beside me, quiet but smiling. Then she moved closer, and closer still; her hand reached the nape of my neck and pulled my mouth down to meet hers in our first kiss. The silence bolted through me like lightning.

VIII.

I stared out the window of the jeep. Uncle Ernie had insisted on offering us much more than advice when we'd called him from La Paz, our craft battered by one of the earliest and most violent hurricanes in recent memory. He drove the thousand kilometers the day we called, and we could barely convince him to spend the night before driving us back to his place. Now the sun was ricocheting off ultramarine waters, as though storm clouds had not yet been invented. But they had, and I found the weather's sudden shift back to optimism almost as jarring as the storm itself. The purity of the blue sky and the mildness of the breeze blowing through the car stung like a slap in the face.

I leaned my head against the window and slowly unclenched my teeth. My jaw was aching.

"Your dad and I car-camped along the coast here, the first time we came down to Baja," Uncle Ernie shouted at us.

He had a huge terra cotta pot strapped into the passenger seat (Aunt Marie wanted one urgently for some reason), so Dylan and I were consigned to the backseat, along with Huey, the dog. As soon as he'd said "Your Dad," I went back to teeth-gritting.

For reasons passing understanding, Dylan leaned forward: "Oh yeah? What was Dad like back then?"

Great. Now Uncle Ernie would tear up and we'd all end up staring silently at the road, trying to lay old memories to rest for the remaining hours of the ride up to Puertecitos.

"Well, he was always up for anything – even when everyone else said it was too dangerous. *Especially* then, come to think of it." To my amazement, he chuckled.

The road dipped abruptly and we rolled with the jeep. These roads hadn't been graded much before they were paved – we could thank a corrupt government for that.

Uncle Ernie kept talking: "The first time your dad and I came this far south, we drove. Like I said, car-camping. It was a recon trip, and we weren't disappointed. The roads were all dirt back then – Dave got really good at changing flats. And we learned enough conversational Spanish to ask the locals where the lobster were or where the waves were breaking big.

"Of course, a few people took advantage of the fact that we were *gringos*. Dave traded his watch for a spear gun one day near Loreto, only to find out, when he went to use it, that the mechanism would lock up whenever it felt like it – usually whenever you had a big fish in your sights."

The more Uncle Ernie talked, the more my nerve ends screamed like they were being pressed with a hot iron. I tried to visualize Dad, young, tan, spearfishing and speaking Spanglish with Uncle Ernie. It worked for about 30 seconds, and then I saw another Dad – blue-lipped and cold, lying on the bed I'd slept at the foot of when I had bad dreams.

I swallowed a lot of times, but the feeling – somewhere between my stomach and my heart – wouldn't go away.

I leaned forward and shouted over the wind and the radio: "Can you pull over?"

"What?"

"I'm think I'm gonna puke." It was the most efficient way to get him to stop, and it turned out to be true.

The blankness that comes when your body takes over only lasted a few moments. Then I had to relive the memory all over again, and this time my mind wouldn't be sidetracked by autonomic functions. The sun glared off the yellow desert, and vultures sketched slow wheels over our heads. *Memento mori*, indeed.

I knelt down like you do beside the toilet bowl and breathed in and out, shaking uncontrollably. I stayed there, my knees pricked by the warm, sharp gravel and arms scraped by a few scrubby bushes, until Uncle Ernie slammed the car door. Footsteps crunched toward me.

He patted my back: "It's okay, Jimmy. You're okay."

I leaned further over and squeezed my eyes shut tight, but the tears came anyway. It was the first time I'd cried in months. I wondered how pain this bad didn't physically rip you apart.

Uncle Ernie tossed me a warm water bottle and I rinsed my mouth out with plasticky water. My forehead was clammy, and my stomach roiled again when I sat back in the jeep and smelled the diesel coughing out of the exhaust pipe.

Dylan had said nothing to me since the start of this scene. I stared straight ahead as I fastened my seatbelt. I refused to give him the satisfaction. But I didn't actually believe anymore that he'd find satisfaction in seeing me break down. We'd said sorry, and I should give him the chance to show that really meant something. Maybe having a brother could again be more than just knowing that a person existed in the world who shared your genetic predispositions.

I glanced to my left. He was looking at me as if he had been doing so for a while, and his eyes were red. He looked away a fraction of a second before I did, running a hand through his already wild hair. Even with his face averted and the rumble of the road under our wheels, the rhythmic rise and fall of his shoulders told me he was crying. I couldn't tell if it was sympathy or if my outburst of grief had triggered his own. Maybe both.

I stared at the roof of the car; the lining was sagging in places, but it had been tacked up with an assortment of pins. The pin holding up the material above my head had the Holy Family on it, their terra cotta faces bright with color. I wondered if my aunt knew my uncle was using one of her icons for so mundane a purpose.

I risked another glance at Dylan. His shoulders were shaking a little less. I thought about ignoring him – I was pretty good at ignoring uncomfortable parts of life. But usually I wasn't stuck in a car with the uncomfortable situation for umpteen hours on a road that rolled and swooped and bumped like a ride at the mid-state fair.

Huey whined at our knees, and Dylan rolled the window down further for him, so that a gale of wind and exhaust swept into our faces.

I'd like to say there was some Damascene moment when the jeep's roof was peeled back and a voice from heaven told me what to do, but there wasn't. Possibly because I already knew what to do. It felt like I was pressing against a Herculean counter-weight, but I lifted my hand from the seat and hovered it above Dylan's arm. Suddenly, I wasn't sure where to set it: closer to the collarbone or the bicep? Was there a particular spot one touched to convey comfort?

Dylan stared at me. He grabbed my hand and placed it on his shoulder: "Are we even related?"

His voice was creaky, but we both laughed a little.

I left my hand uncertainly on his shoulder. I saw myself again, a boy of seven, kneeling down, comforting him after a fall while he whimpered for "Mommy" – but "Mommy" was gone.

I glanced to the front. Uncle Ernie had his eyes on the road. His left hand grasped the wheel like the jeep might be buffeted suddenly by a heavy sea, and his right spun the radio dial, skipping through the tracks of his Anne Murray collection. I thought for a second his ice-blue eyes were fixed on us in the back, but maybe I was imagining things.

I turned back to Dylan. The pale sand and brown hills beyond the window framed his face and gave me a momentary impression of him as a Rembrandt painting – maybe a late self-portrait, both compassion and sadness etched in it.

The last time I saw Mom and Dad together was for Dylan's college graduation. We were all hot and red as boiled lobsters after the two-hour-plus ceremony. The party – at Dylan's and his friends' place – had plenty of vaguely chilled pink 'champagne' and sangria, which our parents seemed to feel obligated to finish single-handed.

It continued to be a sweaty, 80-plus degree day, and it wasn't long until the awkwardly long speeches and toasts began. Dylan's friends' parents went first, and then I felt my stomach clench as I waited, pleading inwardly with Mom and Dad to decide that things had gotten sufficiently sentimental and take a pass.

My dad stood up and said a few words about how fast time passes and how proud we all were (etcetera, etcetera). Then, Mom stood up, wobbling slightly.

"I think you should know," she said to Dylan, Dixie cup in hand, "that I have nothing but affection for your father."

Dead air. Dylan's expression of a moment before was frozen in place.

"That being said, he's the pits. He doesn't know how to relax, and he doesn't know how to have fun. And if I've learned anything from 40-plus-a-few years of life" (polite laughter) "it's how to have a little fun."

I stared at the grass.

"Because, let's face it. Life is short."

I looked up from my cup.

"I remember when my granddaddy died," she mopped at the tears under her eyes with her fingers. "I knew then that it's like they say: life is for the living. Well, Dyl, I've done my damnedest to live, and to teach you to do the same, and I hope Dave and Jimmy can understand it some day."

It took me a minute to believe she'd actually said those words, that it wasn't just overly-sweet sparkling wine going to my head. I looked at Dad. His expression was stony.

Dylan saluted her with his cup. He smiled, casually. Too casually, as if he really was unaffected by her words.

The trouble with memories is, you never know for sure how much you remember and how much you're choosing to forget. Like when someone's trying to jog your memory of a particular event, they keep throwing out details until, like an anchor, one catches. And then you might remember the entire episode, or you might only remember a fragment. And who's to say what *really* happened? God knows, I guess, but He's not showing His hand yet.

A colossal drop in the road was the perfect distraction, but I didn't want to be in the present either – the combination of nausea and humiliation was still pretty potent.

I wasn't sure why I didn't want to remember more of our childhood. Of course Dad and Mom fought. Even before things fell apart. And Dad argued back – what mere mortal wouldn't? What they fought about, who knows? Dylan and I were very young…

I felt the house reverberating to his outraged tones.

It was March, just before Dylan's birthday, and Mom had spent too much money – again.

"What do you mean, it's all gone? Do you even understand the concept of a budget?"

"Dave, not in front of the kids."

"What do you think you're teaching them with this kind of behavior?"

"What kind of behavior?"

Mom played dumb sometimes. Once it occurred to me that maybe she did it as a form of self-defense. That must have been when Dad was at his most raw, after the death of his older brother. Dad hadn't had a good relationship with Uncle Josh, and the sadness was coming out in strange ways.

For example, one time he slapped Dylan in the face for wandering off to see the pigs at the fair, after he had told us a couple of times to stay together and in view. I knew it was important to be able to follow instructions, but I always felt injustice keenly, so I held onto that incident like other kids held onto candy. I remember shouting at my dad that it wasn't fair, that Dylan didn't know he was doing anything bad, but he told me to shut up or I would be next. Maybe that is my real beef with the memory. I kept quiet after that, like a traitor, while the mark on Dylan's cheek glared redder and redder.

The stereo picked up some reggae artist singing "Don't Worry, Be Happy." I balled up my hands to contain the impulse to rip out the sound system. Life wasn't that simple, and it was a desecration to pretend it was.

"Do you think he had time to think of us before he died?" Dylan said.

"I don't know." That was the truth.

We sat in the dinghy, lines in the water. The new sun was bathing the bay. Beyond the horseshoe of sand and houses, sere brown mountains brooded over the sea. We were drifting nearer to the little peninsula of pumice-stone hills. I could feel the boat's rhythm pulling my eyelids down. A drop of sweat gathered at the base of my neck and rolled all the way down my back. I reeled in again, my hands resenting even that much effort.

"Holy *shit!* What's that?"

"What? What?!"

"Did you *see* that?"

"Obviously not, or I wouldn't be saying *what.*"

I felt like I'd just been shaken out of a good nap, which wasn't wholly inaccurate.

"Dude, there's something *big* down there!" Dylan stared over the side.

I felt my stomach turn over: "How big?"

"Bigger than the boat, for sure." Dylan peered into the water some more. "Maybe it's a whale shark! Uncle Ernie said they're back."

My mouth was dry as dust. I stared into the ocean like I guess Jonah might have, waiting for the whale to take him bodily from the boat. We set our rods aside and waited.

"Look! There it is!"

I followed Dylan's pointing finger. For half a second I wondered if he was teasing me. Then I saw it: at first nothing more than a shadow in the water, but growing in size and distinctness as it rose toward the surface.

"Holy shit, it's coming this way!" And what if it wasn't a whale shark? I braced for a Moby Dick-like creature to ram us, or a giant set of jaws to crunch through the aluminum of our uncle's dinghy. Childhood fears of sea monsters lurking in the deep end of the pool or giant snakes coming up through bathtub drains or large fish biting off my toes in the ocean resurfaced, setting my heart thudding.

"You should see your face, Jim!" Dylan shouted. He was laughing – belly laughing – at me.

"What do you mean?"

"We're not gonna die – not yet, anyway. It's just a whale shark."

"That doesn't mean it couldn't capsize our boat." I tried to maintain a detached tone.

I exhaled shakily and told myself to pull it together. I looked over the side again. My heart edged back up toward my throat as I saw the massive shape gliding lazily beneath us. But Dylan was right: the mottled beige and white reminded me of a sycamore tree, but also of those pictures Uncle Ernie had shown us years ago. The huge, rounded head reappeared on the other side of the boat, then its spotted back that seemed to have no end, and, at last, its tail. I watched, mesmerized, as the creature turned again to make the second half of a slow circle.

I felt at a disturbance in the boat and glanced up. Dylan was pulling off his shirt and kicking off his sandals.

"What are you doing?"

"Going in."

"What?"

"Remember? Uncle Ernie and Dad said they used to ride them. You just have to avoid getting slapped by the tail."

I remembered, but at the time of the discussion it hadn't seemed like something we would ever do.

The water received Dylan with a slurp. I watched, my stomach tightening, as he stroked over toward the gently revolving whale shark. I tried not to think about the fact that it *was* a shark – and the largest variety in the world, to boot. True, it had specialized filters instead of sharp white teeth, but it still fell into the same family as the white-eyed, red-jawed predator. I gripped a spear gun, just in case, though I had my doubts as to whether it would pierce its leathery hide, let alone do any damage.

"Look out for that tail!" He probably couldn't hear me.

I reminded myself, down to the tone of voice, of the ten-year-old version of me who had tried to police my younger brother's stunts, including a skateboard ride down the longest (paved) hill in town. I'd threatened to tell Dad, and Dylan had said I was jealous because he could ride a skateboard and I couldn't. So I stayed, arms akimbo, to prove to Dylan and the other boys that I wasn't a tattletale. Dylan ended up with a scraped knee and another sprained wrist, but covered in glory. Dad was certainly not impressed with either of us as we sat waiting in urgent care.

I ripped my eyes away from the circle of water where Dylan had disappeared, and looked around. I couldn't see him. I tried to shove down the panic rising into my throat. It wasn't actually possible that it had eaten him, so ...had its tail hit him in the head, leaving him to sink silently into the deep while I was daydreaming?

I caught a glimpse of a dark mass gliding down and away toward the middle of the bay. I strained to hear again my uncle's stories of riding whale sharks. There was something about avoiding the rear dorsal fin...

I checked myself. Dylan had survived for years without my supervision, and no doubt had tried far more dangerous things. Our time together in that damn boat had probably been pretty up there in terms of danger. Still, I kept my eyes fixed on the topaz water where I'd last seen the whale shark. Moving the boat was no good: Dylan might swim back while I was gone, or knowing my luck, the whale shark, with him on its back, might surface under the motor.

I squinted – I'd forgotten about the sunshine for a second. Then I heard a gasp behind me. I shifted around and there he was, swimming back to the dinghy.

He pulled himself up.

"Damn! I had to get some air or I could have stayed on longer! He was so big, I think he barely felt me."

Dylan's browned skin was goose-bumpy and he still breathed heavily, but he was smiling all over.

I felt a little like I had just come up for air, too.

"You gotta try it, Jim."

"No thanks. I mean, not today. I – "

"Come on. Who knows when you get another chance?"

I shook my head.

"You can't always be so afraid to live, Jim."

"I'm not! I just – "

"All right! I think we can find him again."

Dylan dried his face on his shirt and started up the engine. I stared straight ahead as he began slowly tracing the curves of land along the south side of the bay. I drew breath after breath, trying to get the air down to the bottom of my lungs where I felt like I was asphyxiating. I also watched the water ahead for the dreaded signs of life. Before I could spot anything, Dylan was swinging the boat around and cutting the engine.

"Look! Over there." He pointed off to port.

A huge, speckled shape nudged towards us at about one mile an hour.

"Okay, Jim. Whenever you're ready."

I glared at him, then pulled off my shirt, shivering in spite of the warm sun. I stared at the water, feeling Dylan's eyes on me. I saw again the second half of the skate-boarding debacle, when I'd ridden down the Johnson hill, swallowing yells of terror and an urge to jump off. How I survived was unclear, but I still remember opening my eyes halfway down and feeling like I was a condor in flight.

I eased myself over the side; the adrenaline made my arms shaky. I hardly noticed the water – my whole being was fixed on the snout turning back toward the boat. It was even bigger once you were in the water with it. Judging from similar experiences, I knew that this would not get easier if I waited. I trod water, forcing myself to breath evenly – hyperventilating would be humiliating – until the mountainous back was level with me, then I gave a kick and reached for a hold on that great, slimy surface. Just as I thought I had it, my foot kicked against something and the bottom plunged away from under me. For a second, I forgot that I knew how to swim. Then I resurfaced, coughing, and looked at Dylan.

"Your foot grazed his rear dorsal. You better not have done that on purpose."

"Shut up."

Dylan squinted at the water: "He's coming back."

I saw the whale shark's somnolent face moving toward me again in the water. I waited. The whale shark was coming directly at me this time. Great filters and no eyes to be seen from head on. I swam a little to the left. There was one eye, lower than I'd expected in relation to the pale, soft mouth. The fish was heading under the boat, but I didn't pause to think. Thinking was the enemy at the moment. I grabbed the fin and raised myself onto the expansive midsection. The tail gave a flick and we were off, just as the boat was about to clip my forehead. I wished I'd remembered to take a larger breath before getting on.

A day or two later, we sat under the *palapas* with a friend of Uncle Ernie's, drinking beer. I realized, looking at Dylan, that loving somebody doesn't mean you're suddenly blind to their preposterous habits, like eating peanut butter straight out of the jar or "forgetting" to replace the toilet paper. It just means an endless capacity (or choice, maybe?) to push past those things to who he or she is underneath. I wished I could have met Raquel knowing all this – I might have had some kind of shot with her, if only we'd met now.

Being sad all the time makes you tired. I only realized this in the last few weeks, because I have finally let myself really drink in the good things around me again – like early morning runs out the powdery back roads with the dogs, the buttery tang of fresh guacamole with a *cervesa*, a triple word score in Scrabble, the first jerk of a fish on the line – without tacking on a measure of guilt for each moment I enjoy without Dad. It's like Uncle Ernie said to me as we took turns hitting tennis balls down the beach with his driver for the dogs to fetch: "You shouldn't want to stop missing him, but to stop living on his account would be no way to honor his memory."

It's just us two now. Dylan and Aunt Marie left last week for San Diego. En route, they stopped to pick up Raquel. I'm still fairly ambivalent about that whole saga: not only had she and Dylan been falling in love while I thought she was maybe falling for me, but Dylan also found a way to get back in touch with her and convince her to give him another chance. (He admitted this to me, a few weeks back – the night she agreed to meet him in San Felipe.)

I remember someone once saying, though I can't remember who –maybe it was just a voice in a dream – "So the seasons change. The year, young with spring, ripens into manhood with summer's fruitfulness. Then summer grows old, and loses its hair with the chill of fall. Fall pales and the year breathes its last in the primeval darkness of winter. But the crematory fires are also those of resurrection. For, phoenix-like, a new year rises from the snowy ashes of the old, and we learn to hope again with the green of spring."

I've started to think about resurrection again. Resurrecting a life – even faith. And sometimes, I think about the ramshackle masts and spars that are the remains of *Nelly*, which Uncle Ernie and I are constructing a plan to retrieve from La Paz, and I dream about a fresh attempt at Panama. Maybe I'll give Dylan a call.

***

Made in the USA
San Bernardino, CA
23 January 2020